Masked Mayhem

Maladies

By: London Blue

Dedication

Dedicated to the demons that left scars;

and the ones afraid to show and tell.

You know who you are!

God, forgive us all as we still fail!

Special thanks to my daughter, Laney Letart, for inspiration, repeated readings, and long nights of investigative experiments.

As well as to my daughter, Cassidy Letart, for assisting with my Facebook horror group as an admin and preliminary editor for the book.

My editor, Michele Schiavone, who taught me so much and still answered questions after her job was done.

Also, appreciation to my support system, those who encouraged and stood by me with opinions and advice:

Chip Miles, David R. Musser, Kim Simmons, and the members of my Facebook Group

@WVMaskedMayhem, just to name a few.

Disclaimer

This is a work of fiction. Names, characters, businesses, places, events, and incidents are either the products of the author's imagination or factual accounts used in a fictitious manner yet providing no proof of reality. Any resemblance to actual persons, living or dead, or actual events is purely coincidental. Also, the following content may include but is not limited to drug and alcohol use, rape, kidnapping, human deformities, extreme acts of violence and gore, as well as viruses/pandemics.

Introduction

Still here? Awesome! Let us embark on this journey together. I'm so glad you decided to stay. I hope that some of these writings convey the importance of our youth's mental health during a pandemic. For over a year, we have been locked up and have had to keep our children from learning and experiencing the much-needed social interactions required for human development.

It is my wish among the creepy tales and unimaginable acts that take place in the stories to follow that awareness is brought about by the recognition of an immense need for support and evaluation of mental health. Not just for our youth, but for every soul that has been forced to stand alone.

Our society has always frowned upon people with mental health issues. Yet, this pandemic has created an entirely new wave of mental illnesses that we have never seen before, at least not in our lifetime.

It is time we acknowledge that life sometimes deals people shitty cards. We are not in this together. As some are riding it out in mansions, some are on extended unemployment, while others don't even have a place to lay their head at night. We are not the same, but we all deserve the same rights, opportunities, care, and dignity. Whether these stories entertain, infuriate, or at best raise awareness and concern, then they have done their job.

Acknowledgments

Editors:

Michele Schiavone

&

Cassidy Letart

Cover Design:

T. R. Letart

(Cover designed using Canva and photo editing software - copyright 2021)

Photo Contributors:

T. R. Letart - Four, Five, Seven, and Afterword

Tony Allan Stone - Chapter Three

Taylor Thornton - Chapter Six

Dreamstime.com - Chapter One and Two

Contents

Chapter One – Bystanders

Witnesses

Innocence hoarded in houses
More than a year had passed
Defying laws of distancing
Finally gathering alas

The teens busy necking
Laughing while breaking rules
The ball quickly vanished
But who cares it was the school's

A loud thump caught attention
As a car swiftly passed
Was it the volley flattened
Oh well surely it's trashed

Another loud thump succeeded
This time with crunch and splatter
Holy shit that's not the ball
That's a head and brain matter!

Emma's Attic

Emma sat on her bed, propped up by her fuzzy lime-green body pillow. She twirled her finger in one of the curly locks of her brown hair. She slid her finger inside the curl, pulled it out straight, and chuckled as she let it go. The tight curl bounced back up in a beautifully perfect spiral tunnel. She sent a Chap-chat message to her cousin Brandon along with a video.

I know a couple of these guys!

They were on the news earlier this evening.

They had been caught in the background,

on someone's Pic-Spot video.

Check this out!

While four teen girls videoed themselves dancing outside of their parents' SUV parked in the mall garage, the boys were captured throwing bricks off the third floor onto passing cars below. Brandon replied,

I'm not surprised.

I know the girls that broke into the local hardware store just three nights ago.

They stole thirty-five cans of spray paint.

Great anticipation grew with every ticking minute while

he waited to see what would be graffitied around town. Meanwhile, Emma wondered if her acquaintances would be jailed or set free. What else are kids supposed to do during a pandemic in the middle of summer?

Just like Brandon and Emma, people were tired of being locked in their own homes, quarantined from their family and friends, with businesses locked down. This rampant disease had kept the human race encaged like zoo animals for nearly two years. And just like animals, people with those deep-down animal core instincts were beginning to break out, break free, discarding damn near all the rules of law. Many teens had already found themselves deep in mischief, while a select few had even been arrested.

Once upon a time, the news would report the infectious spread of the virus, deaths, and quarantine measures of other countries, while still giving some rays of light and hope to the rest of the world. The *U.S. News Real* aired a live social media report from Italy. A heartwarming video of people coming out on their balconies and terraces at high noon every day while confined to their homes under strict quarantine regulations. Despite their situation, they still managed to join together in song.

The songs they sang were Italy's National Anthem, a random popular song of the club-vibe mix, and a song of praise and faith in God. Yet, in the face of current homeland fears, no one has bothered to question why our news no longer reports activities in other countries. Have we truly become so self-absorbed that when faced with fear and death, we no longer care for

our fellow man because we ourselves are afflicted? Have we not yet learned that compassion and assistance ultimately yield, at best, gains of love and maybe even additional education on how others are coping and fighting this disease?

This millennial mayhem has certainly wreaked more havoc on the States than on many other countries. We started under lockdown, then eruptions of protests against our government handlings of current issues. Next, our country was divided by politics, family turning on family, friends unfriending friends. Demonstrations turned into wicked deeds of destruction and even treasonous acts. Those who had become infected stormed our very own Capitol. Senator R. Musser didn't make it to cover in time and the mob stoned him to death as if we were still living in Biblical times. His bloody body lay on the side lawn mere steps from the door that would have offered him protection.

The tragedy didn't end there. Between the looting of mom-and-pop stores, historical buildings burned to the ground, and innocent people being mugged, Governor Kimberly Simmons was also attacked. While attempting to board her yacht in the Florida Keys, she was also stoned. Her nephew, an Eagle Scout, tried to intervene by jumping on top of her to shield her from the rocks but was also brutally battered. People were truly losing their minds.

One afternoon, Emma and Brandon rode down to the store with her mother, Lorie. While parked in a mobile-order pick-up spot at the grocery store, they dove into a discussion about the end of days. Lorie began telling the kids how all of this seems to fall right in line with the scriptures. She continued, quoting the King James Bible, which was the very foundation of so many believers, "*The father shall be divided against the son, and the son against the father; the mother against the daughter, and the daughter against the mother ....*" Emma quickly agreed, and then silence fell as the young men loaded the groceries in the back of Lorie's red SUV.

As they pulled away, Lorie finished, "A true believer should be able to recognize the signs. You know I think this disease is worse than any other throughout history."

Brandon asked, "How so?"

"No other sickening sickness, no other mindless madness, has managed to mangle our communities into utter chaos as this Millennial Malady has. This disease is not just infecting the body but corrupting the minds and souls of all mankind. That makes it the worst that humanity has ever encountered," she replied.

Emma chimed in with her point of view, "That may very well be the reason why masks won't help, vaccines are futile, and social distancing is a mere means of further separation and continual division. I mean shit! Nothing seems to be working!"

"Emma! Yes, that's true! But you don't have to curse!" Lorie scolded with a giggle.

As they drove back to the house and carried in the groceries, Lorie was beginning to feel bad for what she said. She felt like she might have scared the kids a bit with her talk of the

end of days. Then she thought of a popular meme that had been circulating. It seemed to have popped up on every cell phone and laptop via social media. It was a photo of a small group of young children holding signs that read, "We are watching! Be good humans!"

So why wouldn't the teenagers and young adults partake in such demonstrated destruction also? They are watching everyone and everything too. Are young people assumed to be immune to the influential contagion called behavior? They are not immune to the current disease spreading over the world, therefore also not immune to learned actions from parents, guardians, and adult leaders. In light of this meme, Lorie felt justified in her talk with the kids.

Although Emma and Brandon had been staying on the down-low of the mayhem in their community, they too were wanting to break the rules. Emma suggested that she and Brandon turn her attic into a haunted house/party room so that they could throw a Halloween party. Her mom had all kinds of Halloween decorations from parties she had hosted in the past. Everyone who knew Brandon knew his dad was a drinker and a smoker of a homegrown substance. So, no doubt, over the next three months, they would have ample time to snag enough booze and weed from his dad for a party. Brandon agreed, and they spent the rest of the evening planning the details and making the guest list.

Over the next month, arguments and yelling erupted in Emma's house between her parents. While she and her mom had been abiding by the stay-at-home rules, her father, Cole, was not. He wasn't just going out to work but was also hitting the bar on the way home. Letting the bars open but keeping the schools and small businesses closed made absolutely no sense. That was his story, anyway. However, some nosy neighbors had tattled on him. They told Lorie that his blue 4-door sedan had been parked at their vacant rental property on the other side of town. She had gone from worrying over Emma getting and bringing in lice, to a deadly disease invading her home, to now her husband bringing in crabs and STDs.

Brandon spent Labor Day weekend with Emma's family. They worked on cleaning up the attic together. As he restacked the boxes from the center of the attic to one end, Emma swept the floor and began pulling out the Halloween decorations. Lorie had been down in the kitchen cooking dinner when they heard her dad come in. All hell broke loose when she confronted him with another woman's debit card. She had found it earlier that day cleaning between the seats in their car. Emma and Brandon listened intensely to their conversation, which wasn't too difficult to hear as the yelling carried right up to the rafters in the attic.

They heard Cole shuffling around in the bedroom. Moments later they heard stomping as he stormed out of the house, slamming the dark solid-wood front door behind him. Lorie called up to the attic to announce dinner was ready, and on the stove, then the bedroom door slammed shut. With a shaky voice, Emma asked, "Are you hungry? You want to take a break and go down to get some dinner?"

"Nah, I'm good," Brandon answered and went back to moving things around the attic floor. Emma sighed, shook her head, then slid a storage tub off a large brown box. Although only the end was revealed, she knew exactly what it was. She had just uncovered the old homemade pine coffin that her grandfather had made for Lorie's parties years ago. Her mood shifted as swiftly as her father had left.

Emma excitedly removed the other boxes that remained on the opposite end of the coffin. She tugged and dragged it until she had it out in the middle of the room. She shouted over to Brandon, "Come here! Check this out!"

When he saw her discovery, he said, "That's freakin' cool as shit! It's like finding a hidden treasure! That's perfect!" Brandon, never avoiding the opportunity to work his bold biceps, took over setting up the newfound coffin. She pulled out the black lights and strands of lights that were masqueraded as plastic orange pumpkins. After Brandon finished positioning the coffin, he took over the hanging of the lights. As he pulled over a step stool, he nonchalantly suggested, "Hey, Emma, think maybe you should go check on your mom."

Emma climbed down from the attic and stopped by the stove first to ensure the burners and the oven were turned off, then continued to her mother's bedroom. She found Lorie curled up on top of a pink and green quilt covering her queen-sized bed. She had cried herself to sleep, leaving trails of smeared mascara along her pillowcase where her face had slid down to the edge. Emma took a blanket from the living room sofa and spread it over her. She sat on the side of the bed playing with her mom's long dark hair for a few minutes. Then she stood up, kissed her on the cheek, turned off the light, and gently closed the door.

By this time, Brandon had come down from the attic. They both fixed a plate from the food left on the stove, sat at the table, and quietly ate together. Brandon could see the sadness on Emma's face but said nothing for fear of upsetting her more. "Would you like some ketchup?" Emma asked, simply trying to break the awkwardness of silence.

"No thanks. I'm good," he said, shaking his head in a quick, side-to-side motion.

As weeks passed and the world continued to go bat-shit crazy with increasing crime rates, Emma and Brandon continued to work on the attic decor. Meanwhile, he had been snagging stuff from his dad's stash to add to their collection of booze and smoke. It was pretty easy to hide it all at Emma's, as her parents were always too busy fighting to notice a jar of shine here and there.

On October 8, Brandon received a new Chap-chat image from his buddy Rowen. It was a pic of a yellow carbon-copy medical form with 'POSITIVE' stamped across the top. Rowen had just tested positive for the virus. Brandon replied,

No shit! Dude ... U ok?

Rowen messaged back,

Yeah, in quarantine! This sucks!

I gotta go!

C U L8ter!

Brandon sent the screenshot of Rowen's pic to Emma.

OMG! R U serious? Is that from Rowen?

She messaged Brandon back.

Yep!

Dude's got the damn plague!

I wonder who else has it ... damn!

Should we call off the party?

Brandon quickly replied,

NO WAY!

WE R DOIN THIS!

At this point, it seemed like the world really was coming to an end. Seriously, Lorie had already confirmed that what was happening had been foretold in the Bible. That's exactly what had been going on with the division of people, even of families, over politics. Not much more to lose now, standing in this new infected, crazy, nearly lawless society. The party must go on, go on for one, go on for all!

Seeing as Cole had left two months ago, Lorie had decided to go out with friends to a Halloween costume party. How perfect was that? Emma helped her mother put together a sexy little Catwoman costume. From knee-high, 5" high heeled bitch-boots, right down to cat eye contacts, ordered online. Lorie was destined to have a good time, therefore so would Emma, Brandon, and all of their friends during their now unchaperoned Halloween party in the attic.

Halloween night rolled in with an electrical storm; how fitting was that. It was an unusually warm night, the sky lit up with bolts of lightning, escalating the excitement and mood for the party. Trying to contain themselves, Emma and Brandon promised Lorie they would not have anything too wild, as they told her goodbye for the night. Brandon began to carry in all the teen-collected contraband they had been hiding in the crawl space under Emma's house, as soon as Lorie left. Meanwhile, Emma started carrying up bags of chips, plates of cookies, and even a brain-shaped gelatin mold.

She had scheduled Door Deals to bring massive amounts of pizzas and wings to be dropped off via contactless delivery for 10:00 PM. Of course, she had to hack her mom's Door Deals account to do so. While she was in the app, she managed to set up a delivery for two bottles of vodka, two bottles of rum, and two bottles of whiskey. She hoped that Trina and her fake I.D. would pass if carded for the delivery. Which, now the world had gone to face coverings like bandits, how could they deny her? They wouldn't see her face, and due to the disease, they really could not make anyone take off their mask.

Rowen showed up first. He successfully convinced Brandon and Emma that he was okay. "I've been in quarantine, and my last test was negative. I haven't had a fever for two days!" Of course, everyone knows you are no longer contagious after the fever breaks. Besides, Rowen had already been given the new vaccine that they claim will stop it in its tracks. Brandon and Emma agreed to let him in, on the condition that he tell no one else he had been infected. No reason to ruin the party worrying their peers like a bunch of overprotective mother-hens.

The next to arrive was one of Emma's friends. Some might say she was a bit on the eccentric side, using today's more politically correct terminology. Old school peeps would have labeled her as Goth, headbanger or, even dating a bit further back, she might have been considered a necromancer. Regardless, between her plump breasts revealed by her low-cut top and the mind-bending 12" tall water bong she brought in, she commanded Rowen's full attention; every part of him stood up in high salute. C.C. was her name, and Rowen could barely speak those two simple letters together without drooling just a tiddybit.

The other guests rolled in one by one, two by two, three by four; it was almost like Noah taking count for the attendees of the ark. Some were allowed in, yet those of the unknown were turned away. At one point, when the doorbell rang, Brandon and Rowen met three old farts at the door. Rowen shouted out, "Ah, hell no! Get the fuck out of here!"

Brandon slammed the door in their face and said to Rowen, "How did those old guys even hear about the party? I mean, they were like twenty years older than any of us! Damn, they must have been at least forty; those old farts need to find their own crib to get lit in!"

They grabbed some 2-liters to take up to the attic, and Rowen laughed, "Must be freakin' perverts or pedophiles! On a side note, did you hear on the news: the state of California is trying to legalize that creepy shit!"

Brandon couldn't help but recall the conversation he had with Emma and Lorie. *Just another example of how bad, how sad, how quickly this country is going to hell in a handbasket. Seriously, WTF is wrong with people? Has this disease caused some kind of mass hysteria, a collective of mental illness, mass madness?*

As Brandon and Rowen made their way back to the attic,

Brandon said, "There is such a thing as collective suicides. Collective consciousness, where one person gets some stupid idea and acts on it, then people in that vicinity and news-viewing area blindly follow like sheep to a slaughter. That's precisely what this malady is, not just an infection of the body, but the political response and restraints on society have become a collective consciousness of pure stupidity."

"That's for sure, brother," Rowen agreed.

Brandon, raising his fist in the air, being a bit more dramatic, said, "Not in Emma's attic! None of that political bullshit, no disparities, no diseased desolations, no negative collectives of any kind, except missing pizzas! It's twenty minutes past 10:00 PM; where the hell are the pizzas and booze?"

The two passed by Emma and she quietly listened in on their conversation. Tugging at Trina's sleeve, she said, "Where are the pizzas, by the way?"

"Good question," Trina said, "Have you got any text updates?" While Emma and Trina dove into researching the status of their orders via the Door Deal app, they made their way to the front porch.

The others proceeded to enjoy the music, alcohol, weed, and other essential party substances. Trina finally got the delivery driver on the phone, approximately fifty seconds before Lorie called Emma to check in. While Trina ironed out the details of the address issues, Emma sweetly talked to her mom, convincing her everything was fine. Lorie struggled to stand up straight and speak without slurring despite the multiple drinks she had consumed. She hung up the phone with Emma, reassured that everything was on the up and up back home.

The girls remained on the front porch as the Door Deal driver pulled up in front of the house. Emma had worked so diligently on throwing the best, no stress, party that she had already missed most of it. She and Trina carried in the stack of pizzas and bottles of liquor. They shouted up to the attic for someone to reach down to grab the new goodies for the party people. Once everything was transferred upstairs through the fold-down staircase, the two rejoined the party.

Emma took just a moment to stand back and take in the fruits of her labors. The black lights looked amazing against their friend's costumes, teeth, and crisp white shoes. Yet, more impressive was the sight of so many people gathered together without all of those stupid face masks. People were dancing together; some were hitting the water bong that C.C. brought. Some were doing shots, and a few were simply holding each other, kissing, squeezing, groping, as teenagers should. They were living for the first time in two years.

Emma and Brandon didn't just throw a party. It finally hit Emma; they just gave their friends freedom. As short-lived as it would be, she and Brandon had gifted a time-out from reality and visitation of what life used to be. No fears, no masks, no gloves, no weary woes. Brandon approached Emma and stated boldly, "Success! Everyone is having a great time! We did it, Emma, we did it!" He grabbed Emma, hugged her so tight, her size sixes lifted off the floor, and her back cracked twice. Brandon sat Emma back down onto her tiny feet, smiled, and gently brushed her cheek with the back of his hand just before he walked away.

Emma joined in the partying; she took a couple of shots of the homemade shine that Mark had brought, hit C.C.'s water bong, and grabbed a glass of rum and pop. Pete scooped her up and spun her around in the middle of the floor. Forced into a position to dance with him, she conceded. A critical problem had developed while she enjoyed the buzz brought on by the alcohol and enhanced by the infatuation she had felt from Pete. Brandon pulled her away from Pete and the others to explain what he and Rowen had planned but, more importantly, how their plan went so awry.

Brandon had confessed to Emma, "You know that a Halloween party is not cool unless there are scares and screams? Well, Rowen climbed inside the coffin intending to randomly jump out to deliver scares that would develop into screams."

"Okay …?" Emma said, with the question posing across her brows.

Brandon explained, "It was my job to bring different girls near the coffin. Then I'd ask the question, have you ever seen an undead? Rowen knew that was his cue to pop the lid open, snarling and drooling while reaching out to grab the girls."

Emma started to giggle, "That sounds funny. Did you video it?"

Brandon crunched his face in a concerned, kind of fearful gaze and replied, "The problem is that the last time I took one of the girls over to the coffin, Rowen didn't come out."

"Ok, so what happened?" she asked.

Brandon proceeded with his story, "I pulled Sadie, the last girl, off to the side and gave her some shine. Then I went back to check on him; Rowen wasn't breathing and had cocaine on his nose and mouth. I think he overdosed, Emma!"

Emma stood there with her mouth hanging open like a busted ventriloquist doll. Brandon grabbed her by the hand and pulled her over to the coffin. He slowly opened the lid to reveal Rowen lying inside, just as the character he had been playing minus the creepy undead growls and grabbing movements. "Well, how do you know it was cocaine?" she asked.

"Well, what does it look like to you? he replied firmly.

She stood quiet for a minute and thought that the two were just playing a Halloween prank on her. So, she reached into the coffin and finger-flicked Rowen right in the nose. He didn't even flinch. "Holy shit!" She muttered. She checked for a pulse; not only was there none, he already felt cool against her hand.

Emma turned away, stumbled back into the corner of the

room beside the coffin. Brandon followed her and asked, "What are we going to do?"

Emma leaned back against the wall, crossed her arms, then began to chew on her nails. "I don't know," she finally said. The two of them stared at the coffin that now encased their friend. Solomon, who had been drinking and dabbing all night, approached them. The two began to quiver, anticipating what Solomon wanted. Tiny droplets of sweat percolated out of the skin on Brandon's forehead. Emma was swaying from side to side just a bit from nerves and a buzz.

A little relief came when Solomon said, "Hey, guys, just to let you know, I'm out! Me, C.C., Rick, Livie, and Hope are going to sneak into the old cemetery on the hill." He grinned big, threw up a hand gesture implying sex, then continued, "C.C., you know that girl has a dark, creepy side. Well, she talked the others into wanting to do some grave rubbings."

Emma snapped out of her trance and replied, "Solomon, you do know they mean epitaph impressions, which are charcoal rubbings, right?"

Solomon didn't seem to grasp the concept or just didn't care and said just as he walked away, "Oh, trust me, I will definitely give them an impression to rub!" Emma and Brandon watched, waved, and said goodbye to several of their friends as they all made their way out of the attic and then the house.

Emma rushed over to the coffin where Rowen lay and sat on top. "What are you doing?" Brandon asked.

"Well, we can't let anyone open this coffin! So, go get me that jar of peach shine or something to drink!"

Brandon sighed, "You got it! One stiff one, on the way!" He smirked and went to get Emma a drink, a really stiff drink. When he returned, Emma was lying across the top of the coffin. Brandon handed her the jar of shine. He sat down on the floor in front of her on the coffin, with a large glass of whisky straight-up.

"Let's get turnt up!" she yelled. The few friends that were still hanging around held their cups toward the rafters, replying as a group, "Turn Up!" Emma and Brandon babysat the coffin for the rest of the night while getting hammered. They both had crashed even before the others left.

Emma was awakened by the sound of her mother downstairs, falling against the dining room table. She slid off the coffin down beside Brandon, who had been stretched out on the floor, and started nudging him. When that didn't wake him, she punched him in the arm. "Mom's home," she said. "What are we going to do?"

Brandon slowly sat up, popped his neck, and replied, "Let's go downstairs and go to bed. I'm seriously hurting." The two went downstairs. Brandon walked into the guest bedroom and fell sideways across the bed.

Emma went into her mother's bedroom and climbed up on the bed beside her. She shook her, "I have something to tell you." Lorie moaned, then rolled over away from Emma. "We had a drinking party last night. Rowen overdosed and is dead." Her mom, drooling like a teething infant on her pillow, didn't respond. Emma curled up beside her and fell asleep.

Later that day, the three of them were awakened by the doorbell. Lorie got up, grabbed a thin pale-blue robe, put it on clumsily, and running her fingers through her dark shoulder-length hair, she answered the door. Emma and Brandon followed her and stood in the foyer, watching. It was a younger man, dressed in khakis and a polo shirt. "Lorie Gibbons?" he asked.

"Yes," she replied hesitantly.

He handed her a large envelope, then said, "Ma'am, you have been served." She slowly closed the door while looking down at the envelope. As she tore it open, she walked into the kitchen. She sat down at the table, pulled out the papers, and began to read. With the papers in her left hand, she used her right to sit the beer bottle back up that she had dropped on the table last night.

Emma and Brandon sat down at the table with Lorie, waiting to hear what it was. Brandon, feeling extremely rough, laid his round, acne-scarred face into the palms of his hands. Lorie broke into a full-blown sob as if a lollipop had just been ripped away from her two-year-old inner child's mouth. Emma anxiously demanded, "Mom! What is it?"

Lorie managed to speak through tears and whimpers, "We have to move out. It's divorce papers along with an eviction notice. We have thirty days to vacate." Emma looked at Brandon, then back at her mom; electrical tingles went through her whole body, like the heat lightning that welcomed in the party last night. Emma picked up her cell phone and sent Brandon a text.

WTF now?

Brandon's phone vibrated in his pocket. He pulled it out, keeping it out of sight by holding it under the table. He typed back, adding a winky face:

Well, sounds like it's your dad's problem now ;)

Emma took a deep breath and exhaled a gusty sigh. Lorie grabbed Emma's hand and said, "It will be ok, baby, don't worry. We'll go to Mae-Mee's."

Lorie's grief quickly turned to anger, just thinking about the situation. *He cheated on me, yet we're the ones that have to leave. Just because that creep knows people in the court system doesn't make this right. There has to be a way to keep him from manipulating the system like this. His day is coming!*

Lorie decided she couldn't get out of that house quick enough, with all of its haunting memories of every fight, his every slap, punch, push and bark. She and Emma packed up everything that mattered and left everything that no longer did in that house. They loaded up her SUV, and she never looked back. Lorie and Emma moved in with Lorie's mother, Mae-Mee. Emma had started calling her that when she was three, and it just stuck.

Emma and Brandon left the attic just the way it was that night. All of the empty beer bottles, moonshine jars, chip bags, crushed plastic cups, and the coffin with Rowen. Lorie wasn't the least bit concerned with anything stored in the attic. *That asshole, the soon-to-be ex-husband, could deal with all of that. He wants it? He can have it!*

Emma texted Brandon,

I feel so bad for just leaving Rowen to rot in that attic

but what else were we going to do?

I tried to tell Mom when she got home that night.

I couldn't very well tell her

during all the new shit between Mom and Dad

Especially now with Dad kicking us out!

She was afraid if she had told her, Lorie would have lost it for sure. Brandon texted,

I completely agree!

Not sure what else to do either

Besides we would be in trouble with the cops

Plus your mom would too

bc she was the only adult living in the house

Due to the temperature outside drastically dropping and Rowen being closed up in the coffin, it took longer than usual for the blowflies to start swarming. However, they did find him. Since it was just an old homemade pine box, they were able to get into it fairly easily. They burrowed into his rotting flesh, feasted, and laid eggs. Poor Rowen was decaying slowly, and besides the flies, his body was being devoured by the bacteria from his very own intestines. As if it wasn't bad enough that the flies, maggots, and other insects were in a feeding frenzy, it wasn't long before the mice found their way into the attic. Ultimately, they found their way into the coffin, too, to nab their fair share of human gobbet.

After Lorie and Emma left, Cole moved back in, and with him, he brought his tiny-waisted, bumbling blond mistress. However, his comeuppance awaited just around the corner of an old-school phone booth. Not only had the neighbors started to complain of a strange, wretched stench coming from the house, but Emma made an anonymous call to the police.

One day when Lorie ran into a store down the road from Mae-Mee's, Emma spotted a telephone booth. *I've seen them on TV but never in real life.* She laughed as she scraped a handful of change from the console of her mom's SUV. She shoved a few coins in the slot, not even knowing how much a call would cost, much less that a 911 call was free. She dialed and spoke softly so no one else could hear but also quickly before her mom came back out. "A teen boy has been killed. His body is in the attic inside a Halloween coffin." She then gave the address of her dad's house and hung up.

Rowen was finally discovered and given a proper funeral. However, because the virus was still so pervasive, only his immediate family was allowed to attend. Meanwhile, Emma's dad had become the number one suspect. Due to his urgency for divorce and quick eviction of his family, he was arrested and charged with manslaughter and contributing to a minor. The D.A. claimed he had provided the illegal substance and then tried to hide the body in the attic, which is why he needed to get his family out of the house as quickly as possible.

What no one realized was that Rowen was still a carrier of antibodies of the malady. All of the flies, mice, mosquitoes and any other insect that dined on Rowen immediately became carriers too. The infection was spreading as those flies and supplemental insects bit other humans. The mice droppings that had been overlooked, as those nasty critters traveled through neighboring homes, were infecting innocent people also with the deadly disease.

Fortunately for Emma, she had an asshole for a dad that kicked her out of their home. Therefore, Emma, Lorie, and even Brandon escaped the probable event of transmission. Sadly, before the doctors, scientists, and researchers discovered that the disease was not only airborne, but was also being transmitted via insect bites and mouse shit, three-fourths of the population of Saint Ellens had already been infected, with one-half of those resulting in death.

Cole was eventually convicted and sentenced to twenty years in prison. Emma visited him only once, with her mom and a lawyer. Lorie went to the prison to sign the last of the documents for the divorce and property disbursement. The decree stated that everything was to be sold and divided 80/20. Lorie, of course, was awarded the more significant sum. Cole clearly displayed he was nothing but a menace to society with adultery and now the murder of a teen on his record.

Lorie bought a new house for herself and Emma, a new car, and found a new love, someone who would genuinely treat her like a queen. She paid for Emma's college tuition in full. Emma carried a double class load, studied hard, and graduated early with honors. She went on to become a virologist and principal investigator. She led her team to discover a more efficient vaccine for the sickness still ravaging the world. Brandon also went to college, passed the bar, and became a lawyer. On an interesting side note, he ended up marrying C.C.

Emma's father married his young homewrecker while locked in the clink. Sadly, he contracted the virus from his conjugal visits with his young bride. Apparently, prisoners and strippers were not on the A-list for the first round of the new vaccines. He passed away due to complications of the disease, and his young bride recovered and inherited everything else that Lorie didn't get.

Chapter Two – Isolation

The Asylum That I Built

I have built an asylum
only I, they keep
yet sole,
authoritative control,
in this claustrophobic confinement.

Prognosis:
Suffocation by emotion.
Restrained: By anger, resentment, strife.
Forever to be denied:
Relief of release, of the knife.

White, dull, walls,
padded with remorse,
construed by heartache, taking its course.
Soldered and raised, from situational debris
Hovering steel, a pin holed canopy.

The floors are too cold, hard,
yellow-stained.
Building formation,
jealousies are pain, soiled
by hate and anger, oh, the destruction.

Light from the Son, forgiving but blinding,
penetrate darkness, that is ever binding,

warmth and pleasures, this brain knows,
casting through, two, tiny windows,
while the conscience bellows.

Consistently stretching, constantly reaching
for positive morsels with firm dedication
too often - those two windows of joy,
are impenetrable from
misdirection.

An exit?
A door. Where is the door?
I cannot find it, I cannot escape!
I panic, then sit. I sit, and I wait,
and then I ponder, while awaiting my desolate fate.

Anxiety builds, it is always growing,
Never calm, in rest, simply annoying,
bouncing between
those door-less walls.
unstoppable, obtuse, like a ping pong ball.

I dig, dig beneath my breast,
to recover some spark to fight, that's left.
While violence does strike
Un-collapsible walls.
I dig deep, for a treasure, a newfound quest.

Unbreakable restraints, birth; failed captivity.

'Round and 'round, frantically searching,
those padded walls, for a door.
Only find myself, always here, once more,
on that cold, hard, yellow-stained floor.

Frailty by struggle, exhaustion engaged,
trapped, like a rat, by consequences.
I still seek, yet I am besmirched.
I must find an exit, I must find the door,
for the windows' sake!

I pull strength from their light
and continue to hunt,
as a lioness, chase the sheep,
and in the still of this asylum, I will, unwavering still,
push on, proceed, for the search.

Quarantined

It all started with balloons and a backyard, ending with blood and an asylum. Approximately one and a half years ago, Aleece saw a chunky dark-headed boy standing beside a big banner attached to the volleyball net in her backyard. Balloons were bouncing in the breeze, tied to the sides of the fence, all along the yard. Her short red hair whipped around her face, framing her freckled nose and thin-lipped grin. She had imagined an entirely different future; when she said yes to the question across the sign that read Will you be my girlfriend? the two fifteen-year-old kids began dating.

Over the next year, they grew very close, from dinners and movies to enjoying family gatherings and holidays together. The two even managed to vacation together at the beach with her family. He bought her flowers and candy, necklaces and rings, romancing her sweeter than any married man could have ever romanced his own wife. At their young age, they had already planned their careers, their home together, and where their two future children would even attend school. It was just like a storybook, or perhaps more so like *Romeo and Juliet* from Shakespeare. As it seems, all perfectly passionate love stories suffer a tragic end. Their love would be no different.

In March 2025, a deadly virus hit the United States. The public was put on lockdown; law-abiding citizens became prisoners within their own homes. People weren't allowed to go to work, grocery stores, or gas stations; only under extreme circumstances and only essential workers were allowed to leave their homes. A person had to get a special permit in order to be on the street. If caught outside without their papers, they would be fined $100 as a first offense. A $200 fine would be issued for the second offense, then five days in jail for the third. This extreme lockdown lasted for ninety days yet seemed like a year. The young lovers were beginning to feel the frustration of loneliness and the longing to touch one another again. If only he could see her face; if only she could hold his hand. Their embraces and kisses, now forbidden, felt like a dark emptiness, a black hole in their very souls.

As time dragged on, some of the restrictions were lifted; however, many were still in effect. A few businesses were allowed to reopen, but it was still strongly advised not to leave your home. A person no longer had to face fines or jail time for not having a permit to go out and were allowed to get the necessities to live. Stores had ropes fastened to poles in front of the entrances. It was like waiting in line for an amusement ride, corralling people like cattle, taking temperatures, checking eyes for dilation, and taking count. It quickly became mandatory for people everywhere to wear surgical masks and gloves.

Just the view of being in a public space became more terrifying than the actual virus sweeping over the world. Plastic face shields, surgical masks, bandannas tied around faces like bank robbers became the societal norm. Everyone was in panic mode, terrified of this New Age plague, but no one gave two shits about what this was doing to the youth's psyche. Just picture what the world now looked like to a toddler. Never seeing a stranger smile, yet instead, everyone's face is covered like crooks and monsters. These masked people should have been hiding in dark corners or under the bed, much less detaining the teenagers like juvenile delinquents within their homes.

When Cupid struck this young couple, he truly grasped at the old saying: opposites attract. She lived on the south side of the tracks, and he lived up on the hill, overlooking those less fortunate. Aleece lived with her divorced mother, Renee, a struggling college student, and an artist. It was difficult during the best of times to make ends meet and keep food on the table. However, this pandemic sweeping the land had created new obstacles, never even imagined. If not for the grant money and student loans they received for her mother attending college, they certainly would have lost everything.

Chad lived with both of his parents in a fine large home, in a gated community. Their oversized decorative door with surrounding stained-glass windows and the grand staircase just inside the fancy foyer welcomed very few. His daddy was a dark, handsome ladies' man. Yet, he was also a middle-aged plastic surgeon, specializing in reconstructive surgeries. Several years older than her husband, his mother was a retired legal aid lawyer, gambling addict, and closet alcoholic. Because of his specialty, Chad's father traveled often, leaving his mother to frequent the local casino. A model family among those struggling to survive in their little community. Chad's mother, Claire, and much older half-sister had made their feelings clear to not just Chad but also Aleece about her dislike for her and her mother.

Several small individually owned shops had already closed their doors and filed bankruptcy due to the lockdown and lack of business. Others were struggling to stay afloat, attempting to convert their businesses to online services with delivery options. Their home state of West Virginia had developed a color-coded map to track and report the number of cases and deaths caused by the New Age plague. Every day became a hit or miss as to whether businesses were allowed to be open or which ones would even survive. On the days that they were permitted to re-open their doors, there were stringent guidelines such as only a certain number of customers allowed inside at a time, face coverings, gloves, social distancing of at least ten feet, etc.

The hardships this caused for businesses and their communities were evident, yet what might not be as obvious was the anguish it created among the youth. Those little mom-and-pop shops such as the local ice cream/coffee houses that the teenagers would gather at were on temporary lockdown. The bowling alley and arcade had to close their doors indefinitely. The kids had nowhere to hang out together, even if they did manage to sneak away from their in-home prisons and parental wardens. Many of the teens would take off on their bikes just riding through the neighborhoods together. Occasionally,

Chad and Aleece would be granted permission to meet at the playground of the local elementary school. However, the last time they attempted to meet there, the Board of Education had chained the gates and left a large yellow sign saying Closed due to Pandemic.

This brings us to the next issue of this tragic time: the schools had also been closed, switching twenty-five percent of the state's total population of underage students to online learning. Many of these students lived in rural areas with no access to the internet. Although the state had very qualified and talented teachers, this massive, immediate transformation was still a fiasco. Most of the teachers wrestled with getting familiar with new software and developing lesson plans for online teaching. Some didn't hold students accountable, so as a result many students began failing semester after semester. The longer this lockdown and pandemic continued, the more the young people fell behind in life-yielding events and activities.

After a year of lockdowns, lock-ins, masks, gloves, social distancing, failed classes, canceled sporting events, canceled dances, canceled graduations, no parties, nor gatherings of any sorts, the pressures and stresses were building as the two began to give up on specific dreams such as college, and the next time they could even see each other. Video calls and Chap-Chat became their only means of communication with others. The government began issuing guidelines and warnings on who and how many people were even allowed in your house. They offered rewards to the general public for reporting their neighbors for throwing parties or gatherings that exceeded the 'suggested' limited number of people permitted at one house.

The tension was running rampant at Chad's house. With his daddy away during most of the lockdown, and with the casino closing, his mother began drinking openly in front of Chad every night. He had been unaware of her habits up to this point. He caught her one night smoking a blunt on the back deck while taking the dog out to potty.

One early morning, Chad saw a man slipping out the back door and a nearly empty pitcher of margaritas on the counter, with two glasses sitting beside it. She had obviously been entertaining someone other than his dad through the wee hours of the night. Also, his sister would often drop her toddler off for them to babysit for days at a time while she disappeared. Subsequently, Claire's new shenanigans left Chad to care for his toddling nephew.

Meanwhile, Aleece wasn't sitting around on rose petals either. She had been arguing with her father and his new wife, as well as her jealous mother. Aleece had just been told she had a gallbladder issue. Besides blood work, ultrasounds, scans, and further testing, she had to change her diet. Any parent on a strict budget understands how difficult it is to eat healthy in the good ole USA, as you can buy a cheeseburger for a dollar, but a salad costs six-plus dollars. This came shortly after Aleece had to have surgery on her shoulder from a previous four-wheeling accident, in which the ATV rolled over on her while she was hunting with her father.

Chad was distraught because he couldn't be with Aleece to comfort her. He wasn't allowed to visit her, go riding bikes with his friends, not even permitted to go shopping for Christmas gifts. He literally became a fixture of his own house while spending his days changing pull-ups on his nephew and chasing him through the house. He was tired of wearing masks and gloves, as if he was a surgeon, following in his father's footsteps to who truly knows where.

The constant bickering occurring in his home with his mother made him feel like a defense attorney in a courtroom. He already had to deal with the house arrest bullshit; now this? His nephew toddling about, forcing fatherly duties on his teenage mentality, was more than he ever imagined. Then the lack of companionship, intimacy, and fighting off the ill feelings from his mother toward Aleece became just too much to bear. He snapped!

One cold night, Chad went out into their three-car attached garage, just wandering around, not exactly sure what he was looking for. He looked over in the far corner at the lawn tools. A rake, lawnmower, shrub trimmers, shovel … *Nah, that would be too messy, and I'm not going to do all the work of trying to bury anything!* He saw the pool supplies stacked neatly on the end of the workbench: PH increaser and PH decreaser, chlorine, bleach, baking soda, algaecide … *What the hell am I thinking? This is insane!* He turned to go back into the house. *She would be able to smell that!* Walking inside, he recalled a research project he had done for his honors biology class last year.

He rushed back to his room at the top of the grand staircase to dig out the poster board from the back of his closet. His research project was on a subject near and dear to his heart. Being able to piss off his biology teacher, who could not say anything about his choice of topic, was a bonus. He sat the tri-fold project board up on his desk, then sat on the edge of the black duvet that held his plush down-comforter on his bed and stared intensely with a grin.

The board held an image, PG-13, of course, but of a young couple having each other in the act of intimacy. On the left panel, there was a large photo of a fly. On the right panel was a picture of a green vial. The title read, Spanish Fly - Aphrodisiac, Medicine, or Poison? He had gone on the dark web months prior to the pandemic and ordered that green vial of this 'aphrodisiac' himself, intending to slip it to Aleece. However, he never attempted to use it because shortly after, his father had come home from one of his trips with research information on this same drug. Only in the data his father spoke of, it wasn't called Spanish Fly but cantharidin.

All of this sparked Chad's immense interest in the drug, and he continued to do more research. He discovered that back sometime around the sixties, doctors used cantharidin to treat warts, among other things. The drug extracted from a beetle was a milky substance found in the male joints that was administered to the female beetle just before mating. Hence the urban legend of it being an aphrodisiac. However, they discovered it had a burning, blistering effect that was useful for removing things such as warts, skin tags, etc. The problem was it could cause other effects such as extreme hallucinations to even madness and death. Because these effects were not published and the physicians had not been transparent, the FDA yanked it from the approved list of medicines.

Chad's father had joined a team of doctors who wanted to petition and regain its approval, as cantharidin could be helpful in so many ways and possibly even combat this new pandemic if given in tiny doses combined with the vaccine. Yet, because of incorrect doses resulting in severe relations to an excruciating death, he found himself fighting a losing battle.

Chad went back online to do a little more study on the vial of Spanish Fly that he had purchased versus the pure form of cantharidin. He discovered that what he had bought from the dark web was close to the pristine state they had used years ago in the medical field. *No wonder it was so expensive.* Now that Chad understood the complete side effects, what was really in the version he had, and just how much would need to be ingested, he realized exactly what he could do with it.

Chad knew it wouldn't be long before Claire started mixing up her evening nightcaps. He Chap-Chatted Aleece, and although he told her nothing of his plans there at home, he did tell her that he would be over soon. "I'm going to steal Mom's car and meet you in the alley behind your house. Be sure to have your suitcase ready. I'm taking you away from all this, and we will be together!"

"Okay," Aleece said shakily, "But hurry before Mom gets home."

Chad planned on taking her to his family's vacation cottage in Mississippi. He had searched online and found out that they could get married there without parental consent. The place was secluded, near the river, and they could hide out there for as long as they needed. He then sat patiently in his room, waiting to hear the blender.

It was sometime around 11:30 PM when he heard his mother downstairs in the kitchen. Only a few brief moments passed before he heard her dump the ice into the blender and fire it up. He figured he would wait until she finished her second glass. Assuming she skipped dinner, the alcohol would have a quicker effect on her. Nevertheless, of course, his goal wasn't for her to get hammered, instead just tipsy enough for her to not notice him slipping the Spanish Fly in her drink. He made his way down the stairs and peered into the living room, where she sat by the stone fireplace reading a book. She had curled up in the leather, tufted loveseat with scroll arms and covered with her favorite beige, weighted, plush blanket. He walked into the room to tell her goodnight and saw she was nearly finished with her first drink.

Anxious to get things rolling, he did something he had never done before. "Hey, Mom, you want me to get you a refill? I'm going in there anyway to get some chips," he offered.

She gave him the stink eye at first, but then with a smirk, pushed her bottom lip up into her top, lifted her wrinkled brow and thought, that wasn't a bad idea. She simply handed him her glass. While in the kitchen, he poured the entire contents of the green vial into her glass and then filled it the rest of the way with the margaritas already mixed from the blender. As he turned to take it back to her, he thought he had better stir it to ensure the Spanish Fly was mixed thoroughly. He wanted to ensure she would drink the entire dose or doses as the vial held more than one. He took her glass back to her, kissed her on the forehead, and said, "Night, Mom. I'm going to bed."

"Oh, ok, goodnight," she replied coldly.

Chad went back to his room and began packing a duffel bag. He snuck into Claire's room across the hall and invaded her jewelry box, grabbing everything of value. Then he slid the heavy metal safe out from under her bed. The combination wasn't difficult to figure out as it was his sister's birthday. *Of course, it was her birthday. She was always her favorite.* He grabbed all of the cash and the small twenty-two handgun. Taking it all back to his room, he packed it in his Nike backpack with some clothes.

As he lay in his bed, waiting for the poison to affect his mother, he decided he should move some of the money and jewelry along with more clothes into a duffel bag. A mere precaution, in case one of his bags got lost, or he and Aleece were separated for a while. This way, they both would still have the means to pay for food, transportation, or whatever until they could rejoin forces.

Chad decided he should go downstairs to check on his mother's progress. He looked in the living room where he had left her, but she was gone. He walked down the hall to the kitchen and found her leaning over the sink holding her chest. "What's wrong?" he asked, knowing exactly the cause and condition.

"I'm not sure, just all of a sudden, I developed a nasty case of heartburn," she answered, frustrated.

He recalled in his research that milk would speed the absorption of the poison; hence he offered to be helpful again. "I'll get you some milk." A little trick that he had seen her do on many occasions after a night of drinking, so he knew she would accept it.

She graciously accepted, saying, "Thank you." Then she gulped the milk.

She no more than finished the glass, then had to run to the bathroom. He could hear the violent episode of exploding diarrhea from the kitchen and began feeling ashamed, afraid, and even a little bit sad for what he had done. She screamed at him as if she knew it was his fault. He took a deep breath and sighed with a grin. While he stood there waiting to see what would happen next, Aleece started texting him.

What are you doing? What's going on?

I'll explain later, just be ready when I call!

Ok, but when are you coming?

The smile on his olive-toned face grew more prominent as he typed his reply and hit send.

Soon!

Claire staggered out of the bathroom and back into the kitchen. Chad asked, "Are you feeling better?"

She snapped back with piercing eyes, "No! Just get out of my way!"

She began searching the cabinets for some type of antiacid or anything that might help, then suddenly collapsed against the oversized marble island. While holding herself up by resting her elbows, she began yelling, "Who is that? Chad, what is that?"

She saw a large man appear in all black; he had to be about eight feet tall and very slim. The shadowy figure swooped over to her. Leaning inches from her face, he whispered, "Time to pay the piper." Then he vanished as quickly as he appeared.

The figure only existed within her hallucinations. Chad had no idea what she had seen, and said, "What are you talking about?"

She began to cry out in agony, holding her stomach. She rushed over to the sink, pushed Chad out of the way so hard that he fell to the floor. She leaned over the sink and violently began to vomit. Margaritas, milk, and whatever that lumpy stuff was that she had eaten earlier in the evening, launched all over the sink and the curtains above it. She stood up and wiped her mouth on a dishtowel.

Chad got to his feet as she began swinging at him and yelling, "Stay away from my son, you crazy creep!"

"I am your son, you crazy old bat!" he finally yelled back. She responded by projectile vomiting all over him. However, this time it was blood. She collapsed to the floor and vomited a third time, again all blood, on his perfectly spot-free, crease-free, white Vans.

He pushed her away from him with his foot and rushed back upstairs. While he was in the shower, her screams of pain echoed through the house. By the time he was done, so were her haunting cries. He bagged up his bloody vomit-covered clothes in a trash bag, grabbed his duffel and backpack, along with the trash-bagged clothes, then headed downstairs. He walked into the kitchen and found her lying on the floor in a puddle of blood, with chunks of food and what appeared to be clots or portions of organs that had been scorched, blistered, and ejected from her body. He leaned over to check for a pulse and felt nothing. She wasn't breathing or moving. A tear fell from his cheek onto her nose as he bent down to kiss her forehead. "I did love you, Mom. I just couldn't take it anymore."

Chad grabbed his mom's keys from the mahogany side-board, which sat between the kitchen and the walkway to the garage. He carried his stuff out to the Mercedes and tossed his duffel bag and trash bagged clothes in. As he slid into the driver's seat, he placed his backpack on the passenger-side floorboard. Then he opened the garage door and started the engine. He called Aleece, "Hey, baby. Wait five minutes, then go out into the alley and wait for me."

"Where are you?"

"I'm on my way, have to make one quick stop, then I'll be over. I love you," he replied.

She ran her hand through her red hair, smiled, and said, "Ok, baby, I love you too."

He backed out of the garage, closed the grey-colored door

via remote on the visor, then pulled away from his home. He was now free from that prison and the crazy warden that held him captive.

What awaited him next was not an obstacle he had planned to deal with. As he approached the gate to exit, his father was coming from the opposite direction. Chad didn't know what to do. He had just murdered his mother, and his father would surely be able to tell there had been foul play. Besides, with him being a doctor, he most likely would have some idea of how based on his own research and interests in the cantharidin or Spanish Fly. *Why the hell was he even in town anyway, much less coming home at 2:00 AM?* Beads of sweat popped up on his forehead, and his hands shook. His heart was pounding in his chest so hard he felt like he would have a heart attack or stroke out.

When his father realized his wife's car was not going to stop, he jerked the front end of his truck over onto Chad's side of the road, blocking the path. Chad slammed on the brakes to avoid collision and began to panic. His father jumped out and started yelling at the tinted windows. "Just where the hell do you think you are going, bitch! You don't think I don't know about your little affair? Roll down that damn window! Is he in there with you?"

Chad, literally trembling with fear, slid his hand in his backpack and pulled out the twenty-two. His father approached the car and tried to open the door. *Thank goodness for modern-day vehicles that lock the doors for you when you pull out.* His father could not get in. He started shouting other obscenities and pounding his fists against the window. Chad leaned back toward the middle of the car, away from the window, and stretched out his arm to roll down the window part way, so his father could see it was him.

"Chad? What the fuck are you doing in your mom's car? Where is she? Is everything okay?" his dad demanded.

Chad solemnly replied, "Mom's dead, Dad."

His father began punching the side of the car, then pulling at his hair and yelling in the middle of the road, pacing back and forth, behaving like a madman. By this time, the lights at the houses near the gate began to flip on, one by one.

"What do you mean she's dead?! What happened?! Where is she?! Was it William? That guy she has been cheating on me with? What happened? Did his wife find out? What happened, dammit, answer me?!!!" His dad was in a complete mad rant.

Chad's father reached inside the car and grabbed him by the neck, and began shaking him. Chad pulled the twenty-two up into his father's face, pulled the trigger, launching a bullet into his eye socket. The blood splattered back into his face as his father suddenly stopped screaming and fell to the ground. Chad looked over both shoulders and checked the rearview mirror for visible witnesses, just seconds before he sped off through the gate.

Just as he told Aleece, he had one stop to make. He drove up into the cemetery. It was dark, and it was quiet; it was where his grandma was. He slowly drove around the backside of the second hill and put the car in park, then killed the engine. He got out and walked over the graves of others to the center of the hill. He stopped at a large angel statue that doubled as a memorial and headstone for his grandma. They honestly believed their money gave them superiority looking down on their small town even from the grave. He fell to his knees, with tears in his eyes, and began to confess to his grandma all he had done. He begged for forgiveness and asked the dead within the ground to give him absolution as if he had been praying to God, Himself. What a sad moment for a young man to be so lost; after being raised in Catholic schools, he still ran to his grandma's grave, instead of God, for comfort and direction.

While hovering over her grave, crying and soul searching, his phone vibrated. He was immediately pulled back into reality.

It was Aleece texting.

Where you at?

OMW Baby, be ready

Well, hurry up it's cold out here

Been waiting already for like 30 min!

I know, Baby, I'm sorry, had something come up, OMW!

As he stood up to walk to the car, a security guard approached him, "Hey, son! The cemetery is closed! You need to vacate immediately!"

Chad, frustrated, began arguing with him. He shouted, "I will visit my grandma whenever the hell I want!"

He moved toward the guard, pushing him out of his way, and the guard fell to the ground. "Wait! You cannot do that! You cannot assault me and just walk away!" the guard shouted.

"You don't want to do this. It won't end well for you," Chad stated calmly.

"Oh, is that a threat? Get your ass back here!" he yelled as he climbed back up to his feet. Chad turned to walk away when the guard jumped him from behind. In the struggle, Chad pulled out the little twenty-two that had put his daddy down, held it against the guard's chest, and fired.

He got back in the car, placed the palm of his hand on the driver's side window, and sighed, "I love you, Grandma." He slowly drove around the loop of the cemetery, then spun out onto the main road, heading toward Aleece's house. When he pulled up at the end of the alley, she began walking toward the car. Chad saw her mom, Renee, coming through the French doors of her bedroom. He jumped out of the vehicle, calling out "Hurry up!"

Renee heard him yell, and she rushed out to the back gate that led to the alley. Aleece jumped into the passenger side, and Renee busted through the back gate yelling, "Aleece! Get back here! What are you doing?"

Chad pulled out the gun and fired. Renee was hit in the shoulder, and she fell against a panel of the privacy fence, then slid to the ground. He jumped back into the car and spun out again. Aleece was crying and yelling.

When he came upon the stop sign of the intersection for the main road, she yelled, "Stop! What are you doing? Have you gone crazy? You just shot my mom!"

He replied without even looking at her, "She'll be fine, I only hit her shoulder and it's just a twenty-two; from that distance, it probably was a surface wound."

"We have to go back! I can't believe you just did that! How did you get your mom's car anyway? What have you done?" she screamed. "Go back!"

Chad turned to her with a blank stare and said softly, "I said she will be fine. We are not going back, too much has happened now, and we have to leave town."

Aleece's face turned as red as her hair as she frantically yelled, "What did you do? Did you shoot your parents too? You have lost your damn mind! I'm not going anywhere with you!"

He became agitated, "Yes, you are! You are the reason I did all of this! So we could finally be together!"

She grabbed the door handle, gritted her teeth, and stated boldly, "I'm going back home to check my mom."

"NO! You are not!" he shouted. He began to spin the tires once again; as he did so, she pulled open the door and jumped out of the moving car. "Fine! You stupid Bitch, but now you are an accomplice to three murders and an assault!"

He spun out onto the main road squealing the tires louder than before. As smoke rolled up from the rear of the car, the passenger door slammed shut. She watched in total shock as the red taillights of the blue sedan disappeared into the night. Running back towards Renee, she found her struggling to get back into the house. She helped her inside and onto the bed, then dialed 911.

The police arrived just before the ambulance, and immediately the officers began questioning Aleece and Renee. They listened and noted what had happened, but Aleece didn't tell them about how Chad told her she would be an accomplice to three murders. When the paramedics began to put Renee in the ambulance, Aleece started to climb in with her. They stopped her, saying she was not allowed to go with them because of the pandemic.

One of the police officers asked, "Is there someone you can call to go to the station with you? We have to take you in to get your actual statement. Otherwise, because of the extreme situation, and you being a minor, as well as possibly in danger, we will have to call CPS."

"No, don't do that. I'll call my mom's boyfriend, Percy. He lives with us. He's just at work right now." she said quickly.

After calling Percy, he agreed to meet her at the police station. She then climbed into the back of the patrol car, leaned her head against the window, and finally let loose the tears.

As they pulled up in front of the police station, Aleece, for the first time, took a close and serious look at the entrance. Although she had ridden past that very station thousands of times, she had never really looked at it. *Wow, I didn't even realize that the police station was actually attached to the fire department. It was undoubtedly a part of the same building. How weird is that? Even more so, why would a police station have three stories of floor-to-ceiling windows on every level? Not much crime in this little town, no proper security measures, as a person could see directly down each floor's hallway. Probably not even bulletproof glass.*

The station's right side, which was the home of the fire department, was faced in all brick with the exception of the large garage door with ample room for the fire trucks to exit quickly. If a person was running, searching for cover from a mass murderer, one would certainly feel safer in the fire department side versus the very transparent and fragile-looking police side of the building. Funny how a person never entertains these types of ideas, whims, or insecurities until face to face with a mass murderer.

The officer opened Aleece's door and escorted her by holding his hand gently over her shoulder blades while softly stating, "Don't be afraid, we will protect you, but you need to tell us everything you know."

Aleece saw Percy standing outside the door of the precinct and rushed into his arms. He hugged her tightly. Then they were quickly dispersed by the officer, nudging them both inside.

On the other end of town, reports were being called in: reckless driving, lawns and street signs being destroyed, hit and runs, and excessive speeding. Chad was losing it; he could no longer hold it together. His thoughts were racing, flashbacks of pictures in his head of his parents, the pools of blood he left them both lying in, cold, dead, and alone. His heart was pounding in his chest like the bass speakers blaring from the cars cruising the strip on Friday nights. Visions on instant replay. Aleece jumping out of his moving vehicle to get away from him, as if he was some kind of crazed psychopath killer. He had no idea what to do next. Fear finally settled into his young bones. Utter chaos happening. All was occurring within his own brain. It was like a hundred different people, with each voice becoming a new part of him. He was fighting himself, his own mind, his own madness! Must be pure madness!

Meanwhile, Aleece and Percy had been escorted into an interview room, where two officers were present and bombarding her with questioning. She told them how Jack had called her and told her to be ready. She told them how she shivered in the cold waiting for him. She explained how they were going to run away together and get married. She then succumbed to a full breakdown of tears and whimpers.

Percy spoke up, "Enough! I'm taking her home!" He threw his business card on the table. "You can call ME tomorrow if you have any more questions!"

Percy then assisted Aleece to her feet, pushing his way through the doors, making their way through the investigations department into the hall. She clung to his arm as they walked down the long, cold institutional-style corridor toward the front desk and exit. As they were leaving the precinct, they approached a door to the left, where they slowed for a moment. They could hear the frantic calls coming in over the air of the dispatch office. Aleece grabbed Percy's jacket to stop him so that she might listen. The calls just kept coming, and units were sent out to the multiple scenes of destruction.

She stood there clinging to him as if her legs would no longer hold her weight; a voice forced its way through a little static and then stated, "Holy shit! Umm, sorry, unit 21 reporting a 10-20 at the Waterfront Water Hole Bar, just inside Jettson city limits. Code 10-35! 10-35! Request backup! There's been an explosion!"

Percy pulled Aleece back to her feet, wrapped his arm around her, and said, "Let's go."

Aleece, with stammering lips, cried, "But it's Chad!"

Percy, practically carrying Aleece down the hall, whispered into her ear, "They don't know that, we don't know that, don't give them any reason to hold you or suspect him. Let's get out of here."

Aleece began to go stir crazy, stuck at home under Percy's 24/7 surveillance. He had even called into work to stay at home with her. Due to the stupid pandemic, they could not visit her mom in the hospital. In light of the suspicion and possible accusations of her being an accomplice, she couldn't respectfully request updates on Chad, either. She felt helpless, hapless, and trapped. She climbed up into the attic, and after an hour or so of pilfering through her father's boxes of 'not important enough stuff to take,' she found his old police scanner. Finally, excited about something, she rushed back down to the kitchen, searching the junk drawers for four not-so-dead AA batteries. *Eureka*!

Aleece grabbed the batteries and disappeared into her room with the police scanner she found in her father's boxes from the attic. One by one, she snapped each battery into place. With each click of connection, she prayed.

Click one: *Lord, please let him be ok.*

Click two: *Lord, please prove he is innocent.*

Click three: *Lord, please do not let him be a murderer!*

Click four: *Lord.* (She shakes her head, then tries again.) *Lord, please forgive him!*

With that last click, radio static waves flooded the room. She quickly searched and found the volume button and turned it down to a whisper so Percy couldn't hear it, then began pushing buttons until discovering the one that scans. She stopped the scan every now and then with each channel on which she heard a voice. Channel 475 - a man's voice came over for a split second, then fell silent. She continued the search. Stopped again on channel 160, where there was some activity, but only reports of the residual effects of last night's local chemical plant fire. Persistently searching to find something useful, she circled back to 475, no activity, just static. Frustration building, her head pounding she finally got a hit. Channel 33.38, an officer from the local precinct is reporting to dispatch; code 10-26. The suspect has been apprehended for possible multiple murders, attempted murder, vandalism, traffic violations, impaired driving, hit and runs, and arson, and is now in custody.

"Chad!" She gasps, clenching her breast. She falls back upon her pink fuzzy blanket on her bed and cries herself to sleep.

Aleece awakes the next morning to the smell of bacon frying. Groggily wiping her eyes, she sits up. She takes a deep breath, enjoying the scent of a pig frying in her kitchen just a stone's throw away. However, she never eats within the first hour of waking up; call it a weak stomach or simply stubbornness, but she either inherited or learned it from her mom. She slowly stumbled into the kitchen to see Percy standing at the stove. He turned to her and gave her a solemn glance. "Good morning, Aleece; please sit down. We need to talk."

She slid a chair out from the table and told him she heard on her daddy's police scanner last night that they caught Chad.

Percy was surprised by her response. "Oh? I didn't know."

She immediately became alarmed and said "Then what are you talking about?"

Percy sat down at the table across from her and began to explain. "The hospital called this morning. Your mom seemed to be improving but took a turn for the worse. She had developed a staph infection which was weakening her immune system. Unfortunately, despite their best efforts and aggressive doses of antibiotics, she was still not showing any progress." He reached over and took her hand as he continued to explain. "One of her nurses tested positive for the Necro Flu and transmitted it to your mother."

Aleece pulled away and jumped to her feet. She began shouting frantically, waving her arms in the air. "Necro Flu? Necro? She got the fucking zombie plague from the hospital?! I'll kill them! I'll call Chad! He'll kill them!"

She stopped for a brief moment to reflect, remembering it was Chad's fault she was in there to begin with. She fell back into the chair in disbelief and in a state of complete confusion intertwined with the most incredible anger she had ever felt. She took a deep breath and then asked, "Is she dead?"

Tears began to fall from Percy's eyes as he slowly nodded, yes. Aleece stood up and slammed her chair into the table. "Are you for real? My mother is dead and you're in here frying up bacon as if we just woke up from a slumber party! You piece of shit! You never loved her!"

Aleece ran to her bedroom and slammed the door. She began tossing things in her room, breaking figurines against the wall, throwing her laptop against the window, shoving the vase of flowers that Chad had bought her off the dresser. After she calmed down for a moment, she began packing a small bag to leave. Sitting on the edge of the bed, she began to cry. *Where the hell would I go?* She flipped on the news and saw the report on Chad. He had indeed been arrested.

Chadwick Liam Parsons,16, was arrested last night for three murders, one attempted murder, multiple hit-and-runs resulting in a vehicular homicide, and mass murder from the makeshift bomb thrown inside the Waterfront Water Hole Bar. Additional charges are still pending. More details to come at 11:00.

She pulled out her phone and began texting her best girlfriend:

Kandy, you know everything that is going on

Just found out my momma is dead

WTF? How?

Chad has been arrested

OH SHIT! You serious?

The freakin' plague is sweeping over us like a tsunami

I don't want to stay anymore

What do you mean?

Where you going to go?

I appreciate you always being here for me.

Do me a favor

Of course! Anything!

Text my Dad tomorrow

Tell my Dad I love him

I'm going to be with my Mom

Wait! What?

Love you girl!

Aleece! What's that mean?

Aleece then pulled out the shotgun her daddy had bought her to hunt with. Just as she got it in position with her toe on the trigger, Percy walked in and kicked it away. "What the hell are you doing?" he shouted. He grabbed her up in his arms, holding her tight. "You can't do that! Your mom taught you better! Besides, I love you! You are my daughter too! I love you! I need you!" They both cried in that bonding embrace. They shared pain, fear, insecurity, but above all, they shared love.

Percy took her to the family doctor and stood by Aleece when she was committed to the psych ward and put on suicide watch. Her dad came to visit, as well as her best friend, Kandy. A few other select family members who shared her pain of loss, confusion, and anger periodically showed up. However, Aleece didn't show any progress until she began receiving anonymous letters.

One day while Percy was visiting Aleece at the hospital, they sat together at the round plastic table in front of the frosted glass window in the commons area. They played a Rummy game, just like they used to play with Renee before she died, when another letter arrived. Aleece dropped her handful of cards and tore into the envelope.

Percy kept asking, "Who is it from? Aleece, what is it? What does it say?"

Aleece just got up from the table, never taking her eyes off the letter. She slowly walked away from Percy without a gesture, word, or nod.

As she read the letter, she continued down the hall to her

room, running the fingers of her right hand along the wall, and counting the doors she passed until she got to her room. Not wanting to look away from the letter, she refused to entertain any distractions from the words on that very, most crucial sheet of paper. She twirled into her room, kissing the letter as she finished reading it, allowing it to slip from her fingers onto the camp-style cot of a bed adorned with a rough army-green blanket. As she gracefully glided across the floor and over to the window, a huge smile stretched across her freckled face. She placed both palms of her hands against the cold glass, protected by black bars from the outside, pressed her forehead against it, and whispered into the air, beyond the candy bar, "I still wait for you, my love."

Chapter Three - The Woods

The Strain

Martial Law

Record Highs

Crime uncharted

Crumblement nigh

Run to the hills

A mountain salvation

The valley infected

Peace in cessation

Few extracted

Horsemen present

Inflicting fate

Graphic evanescent

The Hunter's Son

The morning air was so crisp John could feel it beginning to lay a thin layer of ice over his grey goatee and mustache. His son, Brice, was busy snapping the corner of a candy bar wrapper while treading slowly behind. After dawdling through the previously scouted brush, they came upon the landing they had cleared the month before. They unloaded their packs and began to set up camp. Brice was quick to gather some sprigs and throw a fire starter on them in the middle of the clearing. Once he got a small flame to shoot up from the ground, he went back out to the edge of the site to gather some small logs to keep it going. His father reminded him to get some stones to surround the fire so that the flames could not run off into the forest like an unattended toddler.

As Brice continued to work on getting the fire going and contained, satisfying his father's demands, John finished setting up their bright orange tent. He was glad he had shelled out the extra cash for the easy set-up tent, which only had three poles with connecting pieces. The elaborate raised air mattress, though, proved to be too much to carry in his pack. Therefore, yoga mats would be the foundation for their zero-degree sleeping bags and blow-up travel pillows. Those inflatable pillows were definitely a good buy.

As John made his way back out of the tent, he saw Brice sitting by the fire trying to get a Wi-Fi signal on his cell. John giggled and said, "Grab those kidney bags and let's go get some water." He tossed the rest of their gear inside the tent, and they headed off into the woods. The sun was hanging high above their heads at this point and cast some real soul-warming solar power. They were both relieved to feel a little blessing from God's natural furnace in the sky as they made their way over to the natural springs.

"There is nothing better than fresh spring water filtered

naturally through the mountains," John said as he dipped the first kidney bag in springs to collect water. Brice followed his father's example, but by the time he got his first bag full and capped off, he was taking off again into the woods.

"Where are you going now, son?" John shouted.

"I gotta poop!" he announced loudly.

"Well, don't go too far," John shouted back with a chuckle.

He continued to fill the bags they had brought with fresh water. Luckily, Brice's mother had lined his pockets with some wet wipe packs and other essentials before they left. Therefore, Brice was able to take care of business with no hiccups. When he returned to his father at the springs, he saw that all the kidney bags had been filled. They loaded up and headed back on the trail to camp.

The fire was beginning to die out. As Brice poked around at it, John began to pull out the dehydrated camp food.

"Gross! Are you really going to make me eat that?" Brice asked.

"No, you can go hungry if you prefer," his dad said.

Brice smiled as he pulled his pack from the tent. "What are you so happy about all of a sudden?" his dad asked. Brice sat back down beside the fire and dumped out his pack. Packages of Ramen noodles, canned chicken, Vienna sausages, campfire popcorn, candy bars, and even some marshmallows fell out. With a bold laugh, his dad said, "touché. Break it open!"

After a hearty lunch, the two decided to spend the rest of the afternoon scouting around the woods. Strapping their tree stands to their backs, they headed up the mountain. The leaves on the ground made each step feel as if they were walking up a wet, slick slide; every foothold was a struggle to land. "Some golf shoes would have come in handy," John tittered. Brice, not merely as amused at his father's comment, simply smirked and sighed. The sunlight pierced through the trees, blinding Brice to the point; his eyes ached deep inside and began to water. *Maybe a little more sleep would have helped strengthen those optical muscles to fight off the dangers of the beams, but no, Dad has to start every-thing before sun up. Wake with chickens, and catch the sun, he'd say. Well, who the hell wants to catch the sun, and what does that mean anyway? We don't even have any chickens.*

As he entertained the resentful thoughts in his head, his dad continued to ramble on about some tracks or something or other. Although Brice hates the cold and doesn't even care for deer meat, hiking, or hunting, he secretly treasured this time with his dad. He never admits how much he wants to be there with him. Instead, he grumbles about how he can't feel his fin-gers or toes. John, harboring a secret of his own, knowing how much his son does enjoy being with him, replies, "Suck it up, buttercup, you're a man now, got to provide for the family!" fol-lowed by another hearty chuckle and slap across the back.

They finally reached the top of the mountain, or as close to the top as either of them planned. They unloaded their tree stands and found a dry rock to park their rumps on. Brice chose one a little further away because it lay in the warmth of the sun. John pulled a bottle of water from the side pouch of his stand and offered his son a drink. Brice shook his head no, and John began to shoot off the questions. "So, what do you think about your mom's new boyfriend?"

"Dad, I don't want to talk about Mark right now." He was getting a bit aggravated.

"Okay, Okay, just want to make sure he's good to you," John continued.

"Yeah, he's alright, I guess. Can we talk about something else now?" Brice asked.

John looked around, then back over to him. He sat quietly for a moment admiring the handsome young man his son was becoming. *Wish I still had dark thick hair like that. Wish I still had his mother in my life.*

"So, which tree do you want?" He finally spoke, diverting his thoughts.

"The one here in the sun," Brice replied.

"Well, let's get it done!" John said.

The two grabbed their stands and began to climb up their individual picks of the tall trees. Once their tree stands were safely secured in the trees, they climbed back down. They were sure to remove the screw-in-steps as they went, so they didn't leave easy access for someone else to get in or take their stands. They trekked back down the hill to the campsite. After the fire was rebuilt, they roasted some hot dogs and opened a can of baked beans.

During dinner, John once again tried to push his son to talk about his mother and her boyfriend. Brice jumped up to his feet in anger, tossed his hot dog into the fire, and yelled, "I told you I don't want to talk about them!"

John stood up and tried to apologize, but Brice had taken off through the woods before he could get anything out. John called out to him, "Brice! Brice, stop! You can get lost out here, and there are dangerous animals." He started to follow him, as he continued to yell to him, "Brice! Dammit! Get back here!" But he completely ignored his dad and began to run. John lost sight of him.

He kept looking for his son all through the night with no luck. It was already way beyond midnight. The cold air pierced John's bum knee like icepicks, making it extremely difficult for him to walk. As much as he wanted to keep searching for his son, he had to make the tough decision to turn back toward camp. *I'll just get rested, then start again at first light. Then I can put my knee brace on, too.*

Brice had certainly gotten himself lost. He had circled halfway around the mountain, dipping down into and crossing a deep valley. Then he made his way about halfway up the other mountain, but he was too weary to continue. Fortunately for him, he ran across a large rock protruding from the side of the mountain. He decided that would make for somewhat of a decent shelter for the night. Shoving the leaves up under the rock, he formed a temporary bed. He curled up on the leaves, keeping his back against the mountain, and it wasn't long before he fell asleep.

The next morning, while the sun began to thaw out his face, he woke up to something poking at his knees. He jumped up, fearing the worst, recalling what his dad had told him about bears in those woods. He sighed with relief when he saw a girl about his age, with a long dark blond braid hanging over her left shoulder. She was squatting down in front of him, holding a stick. His puzzled look must have been unsettling as the girl brought her finger up to her plump lips and made the shhh sound. "Are you okay?" she whispered.

"Yeah, I'm fine, just seriously cold and hungry," he replied in a meager voice. "Wait. Why are we whispering?" The girl made the shhh gesture again, stood up, and motioned for him to follow her.

Brice got up, rubbed his legs several times to warm them, and stumbled along behind her. "Where are we going? I thought you might be taking me back to my campsite. Hello?" The girl would occasionally turn back to him with a smile but said not a word; she just motioned for him to continue following her. He finally stopped and sat down on an old log. They had hiked through the woods for what seemed like at least a half-hour. He was tired, cold, hungry, and quite frankly getting mad. "I'm not going any further until you talk to me!" he exclaimed.

She sat down beside him and softly and slowly spoke, as if the words were struggling to come out of her mouth. "I'm sorry, I do not know exactly where your campsite is. We are almost to my home. I can get you food and something to warm you."

Crossing his arms in front of him, he embraced himself

and began rubbing his muscular but thin biceps and shoulders to create friction. "That sounds good. How are you not cold? You haven't shivered once," he said.

She slid over closer to him to share her body heat and started to explain. "It was about four years ago; I was twelve when my family contracted the fever."

With a shocked expression on his pale face, he interrupted, "The fever? You survived the fever? How?"

She shrugged her shoulders and continued, "I'm not sure. You see, when the fever broke out, and people started rioting and looting, my family moved up here in the mountains. My father and grandfather said we would be safe here. But we were attacked. The men in our family had to fight off many stragglers who tried to break into our cabins and steal from us. There were some with the fever who came into our borders, and they infected my grandfather and little brother. It wasn't long before it spread throughout our whole family, including me." She stood back up and motioned for him to get up. "We really should get going."

Brice rose to his feet but was still hesitant. The girl tugged on the shoulder of his coat. "Fine," he sighed, and continued to follow behind her like a lost sheep to the slaughter. "Well, that still doesn't explain how you all survived it. Did your family find a cure? Finish the story!"

She flashed him a secretive smile and said, "Well, we've heard that the vaccines were working."

"Yeah," he agreed, "but it's not completely gone, and there are strange side effects from it. Last week, I heard on the news that one woman had developed bone cancer in the arm she was vaccinated in. They claimed it was from the vaccine. So, if your family has found a natural cure here in the mountains, you should share it."

The girl just kept walking, ignoring his response, and

he kept following her. They came upon barbed wires twisted around large trees that created three tiers of fencing. "Wait, I don't even know your name. What's your name?" Brice asked.

"My name is Isis, and it would be best if you wait outside the fencing until I get back. I'll only be a few minutes." Then she squeezed through the fencing and disappeared among the trees. He slid down against one of the trees that was still standing in the sunlight, rubbing his hands together.

Isis was gone for a long time. Brice began wondering if she was even coming back and thinking he should maybe try to find his way back to his campsite. His father must be distraught. Isis finally reappeared. She was carrying a blanket made from a bear hide and a basket of food. "Where the hell have you been?" he shouted.

She laid down the items she had brought beside him, held her finger against her lips, and said again, "Shhhh."

He pulled the bear hide over his lap and dove into the basket of food like a shark tearing apart its prey. While he ripped into the odd tasting meat, Isis asked, "So, you know my name, what's yours?" He looked up, wiped his mouth on his sleeve, and said, "Oh yeah, I'm Brice, and thank you for all of this."

Isis began packing everything back up in the basket and said, "You're welcome, now let's go!"

He stood up and replied, with a troubled brow, "What? Why? I thought we were safe here?"

She reached down and grabbed the bear hide, then replied, "I am. But I don't think you are. Let's go." She tugged at his arm, trying to make him leave with her.

He stood firm this time and asked again, "Why? What's going on?"

Isis took a deep breath, sighed impatiently, and then spoke with great urgency, "There is a reason, I didn't tell you how we beat the fever. I'm afraid you may be in danger. Please, let's just go, and I'll explain later."

He wrinkled his forehead, scrunching his brows until they nearly met in the middle, and let out a low growl. "Fine!" Then he picked up the basket of food and began to follow once again.

The two didn't get far before he became too agitated to keep going. He stopped and just stood there watching her. She realized he wasn't walking but kept going while she told him there was a cave just ahead. He kicked a large rock with his boot and shouted out in pain, but he proceeded on. They finally came upon the cave she spoke of. She had turned it into some kind of strange clubhouse. It was still fairly close to their compound and had been adorned with deerskin rugs, lanterns, a few books, and even an old wind-up record player with four or five vinyl records. Brice made himself at home quickly, as he was exhausted, cold and angry. Isis began to build a fire in a small pit made with stones like he had built back at his camp with his father.

Once the fire got going, he moved closer onto one of the deer skins beside her. While pulling one end of the bear hide over his legs, he asked, "Okay, so now spill it. What's going on?"

She spun around to face him, pulled her thin legs in close in a crisscross position, and began to explain. "Well, you asked how we beat the fever. I honestly didn't know, up until about a month or two ago. Time has a way of slipping by up here."

She handed him some jerky, trying to figure out a way to tell him of her family's dirty little secret and worse, what she had witnessed at their compound. She tried to buy herself some more time so that she could gather her thoughts. Isis got up and walked over to the rear of the cave. She showed him the fresh spring water running down the back wall as she caught some with a metal camp mug.

"Quit stalling and keep talking," he demanded, accepting the cup of water while running his fingers over her small hand wrapped around the mug.

She sat back down in front of him, resuming her crossed-legged position, interlocked her fingers, rested her elbows on her knees, and leaned her forehead against her thumbs. "When we were attacked by the stragglers coming up the mountain, my family was forced to defend themselves and they shot them." She looked up at him, gauging the level of judgment based on his facial expression. He appeared calm, so she continued. "We had been struggling for months to survive. That first winter was very hard, and the game was scarce. So ...." She placed her hands on each side of the deerskin that she was sitting on, repositioned herself into a straight-up proper posture, tightened all of her muscles, then spit out in a quick burst, "We ate them." A person could have driven a dump truck in the gaping hole that seemed to have swallowed Brice's face.

"You what?!" he howled.

"We didn't have a choice!" she yelled. "We were starving! We had already lost my grandma, and since the outbreak occurred in late October, we didn't have time to plant and harvest anything." She continued defending her family's actions. "All we had was what we managed to grab on our way out of town, which wasn't much. Besides, it wasn't like we killed them to eat them! They attacked us!"

He eased back a bit with a judgmental look on his face and asked slowly, "Is that what this weird tasting meat is that you gave me?"

Tilting her head to the side, she replied, "Well, not that," pointing to the chunk of meat that had been wrapped in wild grape leaves. "But the jerky is." She cringed, awaiting his response.

He rubbed his face with both hands and then asked, "So, how does this explain how you beat the fever and why you thought I was in danger?"

Isis told him how those who had been infected suddenly started getting better after they ate the flesh of the men that had attacked them. "Grandfather seems to think that the men had been infected with the fever when they died. Then when we ate them, the sustenance created some type of natural vaccine. You know, like, how they put the actual flu virus in flu shots?"

Brice squirmed a bit, then stated boldly, "Yeah, but that strand of the flu is a dead agent!"

Isis shrugged her shoulders at him and answered, "Well, so were those men!" They sat together in silence as the sun began to set, watching the beautiful rays of orange and red crawl across the floor entrance of the cave and disappear.

Isis lit one of the lanterns and laid down. Brice laid down beside her and offered to share the bear hide as a blanket. She told him she was fine, and he inquired again, "Yeah, about that?"

Speaking softly as she began to doze off, she said, "I suppose it was a side effect of eating the infected." She rolled over with her back facing him and fell to sleep. He lay there a while, studying everything he had just learned. He could understand their dilemma and why they did what they did. After chewing on it for a while, he figured if he and his dad had been in the same position, they might have done the very same thing. He, too, fell off to sleep, thinking about his dad and hoping he was okay.

The following day Brice told Isis that he needed to find his way back to his campsite because he just knew his father was frantic by now. He sat up, grabbed some jerky from the basket, and then readjusted the laces on his boots.

"Wait!" Isis shouted. "That is like an all-day hike."

He gave her a scowl as he replied, "So! I need to find my dad!"

Isis stood up in front of the cave entrance before him and hesitantly spoke, "He's not at your camp."

Angrily jumping to his feet, he asked, "How do you know?"

She fearfully replied, "Because he's at ours."

He began yelling. "What do you mean he's at yours? Why didn't you tell me? Why did you bring me back out here to this damn cave if my dad is sitting in one of your nice cozy cabins?"

She held out her hands, palms down, and motioned for him to calm down. "You need to lower your voice. Your dad is at our compound but not in one of the cabins. He's been captured. My family must believe he is another infected straggler. If you go in there, they will lock you up too. So don't try to be a hero. You will get killed, and so will your dad. At least right now, he's alive."

Brice, even madder than hell, said, "Is that why you led me to your compound, to become your family's next hundred plus pounds of jerk?"

She approached him slowly and tried to take his hand, but he pulled away. He pushed her to the side and told her he was going after his dad. "Wait. I was trying to help you. I like you and thought maybe you and your dad could stay with us. I had no idea they had captured him when I met you!"

Ignoring her pleas, he continued out of the cave. "You will never make it past the fencing, and there are boobie traps everywhere! Wait! I'll help you!" she yelled.

On their walk back to the compound, he asked, "How can I even trust you? I mean, you eat people!"

Isis, who had been trailing behind him, rushed up to his side and grabbed his arm. "Because I didn't have to tell you where your dad was. I didn't have to bring you food. I certainly don't have to risk my neck right now, trying to help you get your damn dad!" That seemed to shut him up for the time being.

When they approached the barbed wire fencing again, she motioned for him to be quiet and follow her around to the other side. She whispered in his ear, "Over there is easier access. There aren't as many traps set coming up between the cabins, so none of the children would get hurt."

He looked at her, perplexed. "I thought just your family lived here?" he asked.

"Well, we have been here for over four years now. It started out as just my family, then different friends joined us over time, and they, in turn, brought others. There are a lot of people here now, which means a lot of mouths to feed. Unfortunately, people are tired of leftover crops already, and again this year hasn't proved all that prosperous in hunting, which may be why they took your dad. We can't afford competition for game and if they think your dad is infected, he's not just food but also a vaccination for the newcomers and toddlers."

Brice grumbled under his breath, knowing he had to keep his cool in order to find and rescue his dad. They darted out from among the row of log cabins across the field and ducked down behind a well. He could now get a good idea of the layout of the compound. They waited until two women with a small child passed by, then rushed over to the corn stalks. "Your dad is locked up under that canopy of brush across from the pond," she whispered while pointing to the right of the garden. He nodded and sprang out from the cornstalks like a cricket escaping a bathtub drowning.

He found his dad locked up in what appeared to be some type of homemade dog kennel. He grabbed the metal poles, reaching for his father's hand. "Dad! I'm here!"

His father inched himself over to the side and placed his hand on his son's. His speech was muffled by his low tone and the hoarseness of his voice. "Brice. Oh, thank God, you're safe. How did you find me? Are you okay?"

As Brice scurried around the other side to the door, he began fiddling with the lock. "I'm fine. Let's just get you out of here."

Frustrated, he slammed the lock against the cage and reached for his hand again. "Don't worry; I'll find a way to get you out." When his dad repositioned himself to reach his hand again, he revealed the end of a bandage under his sleeve. Just as Brice began to ask what had happened, Isis snuck up behind him.

She squatted down with her hand on his shoulder and whispered, "You have to be quiet. They have started shaving layers of flesh from his arms and legs to make more jerky. I guess they figure if they don't kill him, it's not murder. However, they can keep him alive and still create their form of the vaccine and food piece by piece. That way, when he heals, they can do it again and again--an endless supply of protein and medicine."

Brice and John both looked at her with complete horror. "You people are freaking crazy!" John belted out.

"Shhhh! She's trying to help us." Brice scolded his dad while holding his finger perpendicular to his pale lips.

Isis pulled a tiny rusted key from her pocket. "Sorry it took me so long, but I went back to the cabin to snatch the key off dad's chain." She handed the key to Brice, and he unlocked the cage.

John crawled out of the cage, and the two teenagers helped him up. "Wait," Isis whispered quickly, "maybe we should wait until the sun sets. Since they have literally stripped his skin, it will be too painful for him to move fast enough to get out without being spotted."

Brice looked to his dad, and John nodded at him in agreement. So Brice asked Isis, "Well, is there someplace close by that we can hide out until then? Just in case someone comes in the meantime."

She thought for a moment, "If we can get up that little hill behind the brush here, there is an old shed that we store extra firewood in. We could wait inside, but it would be cramped."

John grunted as the pain was horrible just standing there, then said, "Let's go. Let's go."

Once Isis helped Brice with John to the shed, she told them that she would go back to her cabin. She figured they had been looking for her, so her return would be a distraction from their now escaped prisoner. Besides, she would be able to eavesdrop on any conversations regarding John. "I'll be back just before sundown, so we can get outside of the compound before they bring his dinner." Isis left the two and headed back to her family cabin.

Brice helped his dad get settled inside the tiny shed against a stack of wood. There was barely enough room for Brice to sit beside him against the door. He asked, "What happened? How did they capture you?'

John replied in a weak voice, "I was out looking for you when they found me. They asked me what I was doing on their mountain. I told them we had come up to do a little hunting and that you got lost. They pulled out guns and a couple of homemade spears, then said we had to leave immediately. They claimed this was all private property. When I said I wasn't leaving without you, they began threatening me. As they drew in closer, forming a circle around me, I just knew they were going to attack. I shouted I was infected with the fever, thinking that they would back off. Instead, they grabbed me and brought me here."

"Dad, that was the biggest mistake you could have made!" Brice replied, then told him everything that Isis had said.

John's jaw dropped in shock, then he continued, "Well, I guess that explains why they were flaying my flesh!"

Brice reached over to his dad's arm and asked, "Let me see?"

John shook his head, laid his head back against the wood, and closed his eyes. "Let's just get some rest for now."

Meanwhile, Isis explained to her parents how she had been out tracking some type of weird, mutated-looking bear prints. She took the time to elaborate on every detail; how the bear track was missing two toes on each front paw and was much narrower than a typical track. Her father, intrigued with this tale, kept asking questions such as location and depth. Isis very wisely told him she had been scouting on the opposite side of the mountain, hoping her father would take a team out to look for it. She grabbed some grapes off the long table hewn from a log and stood in front of the stone fireplace. Popping one grape at a time in her mouth, she grinned as her father grabbed his gun and said he would go check it out.

As her mother went into the kitchen to prepare dinner, Isis grabbed the bag of grapes and some muffins off the table. She shouted back to her mom as she went out the door, "I'm going with dad to show him where I saw those tracks! Love you!" Then she pulled the rustic cabin door closed behind her and headed back up the hill to the shed to get Brice and his dad. The three of them made their way around the traps and other contraptions exiting through the barbed wire fence and compound.

Once Isis felt confident that they were far enough away, they stopped to rest against a large pine tree. She searched around until she managed to find a large, sturdy branch that would suffice as a cane for John. She took it back to where they had been sitting, pulled out a buck knife, and sliced off the tiny sprigs that were hanging on for dear life. Occasionally she would stop and rub the sap off of her hand onto her jeans.

She sat down beside Brice and whittled away at one end, smoothing it down to grip more comfortably. Then she asked, "How much did they take?"

John knew exactly what she meant, sighed, and replied, "Quite a bit. They flayed three rows from my hip to my knees on each leg and two strips from each shoulder to each wrist."

Isis interrupted while handing them the bag of muffins and grapes, "Here, you guys need to eat to keep up your strength."

Brice took the bag and handed his dad the largest muffin while he dined on some grapes.

She looked to John to inquire again, "Is that all?"

John leaned forward slightly, pushing his shoulders back to release his shirt and coat from the wounds. "No, they took some off my back. I'm not sure how much, but it feels like most of it."

Isis saw that John was growing weaker and quite pale. "We should get going. We need to get him to the cave, and then we can check and redress his wounds," she said as she stood up and offered John her hand to help him up.

The three struggled for close to two hours but made it to the entrance of the cave. Once inside, Isis told Brice to help his dad get undressed to reveal his wounds. While he did so, she built a fire to keep them all warm. John was starting to shiver; the fear of hypothermia setting in was real. The excessive blood loss, lack of protection from his absent skin, and the cold temperature were all placing him on the brink of death.

Isis and Brice removed the blood-soaked bandages that her community had put on him. She pulled out a spray bottle and began saturating his back. John yelled out, grabbed his heavy green jacket tight, then clenched it between his teeth. Two strips of skin were removed along his back from his shoulders to his waist, approximately five to six inches wide.

"What is that?" Brice asked aggressively. Isis stepped back, instructed John to turn his back to face the fire so the solution could dry and set. Glancing over to Brice, she replied, "It's a homemade solution that we use for injuries. I'm not sure exactly what is in it, but I know there is aloe, witch hazel, and olive oil. This stuff works amazingly. It will disinfect it as well as soothe and heal."

After a few moments, Isis sprayed John down again with the solution, then explained, "By allowing it to air dry, it will form a barrier, so to say, between the wounds and the new bandages, and this will help stop the bleeding and keep out infection." After she redressed all of his wounds, Brice helped his dad put his clothes back on. She tossed the old, bloody bandages into the fire and then pulled out the basket of meat and dehydrated fruit that they had left earlier.

While sitting around the fire eating, Brice took a large bite of the jerky and then laughed. "Well, at least we know we aren't eating Dad. They haven't had time to prepare him yet." They all chuckled a bit, then he continued more seriously, "You know, the problem is, Dad and I are not infected with the fever. Dad said he told them he was, hoping they would back off. So they skinned him for no reason."

The expression on Isis's face turned sour; she appeared as if she was about to cry. "I'm so sorry they did this to you. They told me the only reason they had done it in the past was that those people had attacked us, and it was in defense that they killed them. As far as…" She cleared her throat and wiped a tear from the corner of her eye. "As far as eating people, we were literally starving up here."

John reached over and patted her on the knee, saying gently, "It's not your fault." Then he lay down on his side by the fire. Brice also lay down with the top of his head nearly touching his father's. He grabbed his dad's hand and softly whispered, "I'm so sorry, I love you."

John squeezed his hand and replied, "I know, son, it's okay. I love you too."

Isis began to hum as she too lay down, across the fire from them. Her hum turned into a soft melody of *Amazing Grace*. John smiled as he fell asleep.

Brice looked to Isis with a serious gaze and said, "I need you to stay here with my dad. At first light, I'm going to find my way back to our truck and get help."

Isis nodded, "Of course."

Just as he said, when the sun began to beam into the entrance of the cave, Brice got up and prepared for his journey to look for help. He grabbed the bag that Isis had brought out of the compound with them, leaving everything except for one muffin and some grapes. He also picked up a small chunk of the meat from the basket and headed out of the cave before the others awoke. He ate the muffin and tied the bag with the remaining items around his belt on his way around the mountain. He slid the buck knife that Isis had laid out for him the night before down the side of his boot.

Brice had already been gone about two hours before Isis woke up. She stoked the embers in the fire and placed a couple more logs on. While she collected some of the spring water in a pan and put it over the fire, John began to stir. She knelt beside him and asked if he was okay. His body shivered, and she knew he was getting much weaker. She pulled the bear hide over him and offered him some water. He managed to raise himself up onto his elbow, take the metal cup, and supped, just a little, but did not speak.

"I'm heating some water so I can make you some tea. These leaves also have natural healing elements and should help combat infection." She continued, "But you should try to eat some jerky. It does have some type of antibodies against the fever, so I'm sure it must have some sort of healing agent as well. I'm not sure what all they used when they dehydrated it. Dad had some kind of special seasoning concoction that he soaked and basted it with." She handed him a piece of jerky.

"I don't know," he said reluctantly while staring at it in his hand. "Just knowing I am eating another human." John wrinkled his face up into a snarl.

"Please, eat it. Don't think of it like that. Besides, it was mixed with deer meat too. So just focus on the deer and try not to think of the other ingredients."

He managed to yank a piece off with his teeth. As he chewed, he looked around and saw his son was gone. "Where is Brice?"

Knowing the news would upset him, she spoke gently. "He went to find your truck and get help."

John dropped back on the ground, grabbed his face with his dirty, calloused hand, and sighed.

Meanwhile, back at the compound, they had already discovered that John escaped. Seeing that Isis had disappeared again and the lock had been opened with the key, they realized she must have helped him. Her father was furious, figuring her story of the unusual bear tracks was just a pretentious ploy to keep them off their heels. Another search party was formed to find her and their escapee equipped fully with handheld walkies and weapons. They could not let that man get away and reveal their location, as everything they had built would be destroyed.

Brice spotted their stands still perched in the trees above on the other side of the mountain adjacent. He had finally found his way back to their camp. He knew the walk onto the truck wasn't much further. He climbed into the tent, took off his coat, and paused for a moment to rest. He opened one of the energy bars and drank some water. As he dug through his father's pack, searching for the keys, he heard crunching just off the path. Chills ran up his spine as he listened to his dad's voice casting out from his memory bank, shouting about the wild animals in the woods.

He pulled the hanging flap away from the corner of the screen and peeked out of the back window. His fears materialized before him, a hefty black bear with dinner on his mind. Brice gasped for breath as he watched the bear move closer, sniffing around the perimeter of the campsite. He went back to digging down into his dad's pack and grabbed the keys. Holding them tightly in his hand, so they didn't rattle, he peeked out again to see exactly where the bear had wandered, with no sight of it. He sat quietly for what felt like an hour, and with no further scuffling heard, he slowly crawled out of the tent.

Brice scanned around the edge of the campsite and still

saw no signs of the unwelcome visitor. He put on his spare wind-breaker, slid the keys in the pocket, zipped it closed, and headed down the hill toward the truck. He was trying to stay alert but couldn't stop his mind from wandering off regarding his dad. The guilt was gnawing at him like mice at the drywall of his dad's old house. *If I had just stayed at the campsite and told him what I thought of Mom's boyfriend. Suppose if I had just told him that the guy was a douche and that I hate him. If I had just talked to him, they wouldn't be in this situation.*

The sun was beginning to set, and he had to make up some time for getting lost on the way to the camp. As he picked up speed, he tripped over a root on the path and slid down the side of a knoll. Traveling down the remainder of the hill on his back-side, he stopped only when he hit the middle of a mudhole. His clothes soaked with mud, he could already feel the chill. But on the positive side, at least the mud would mask his scent from the bear. Or so he thought.

When he stood back up, the bear was standing over him on his back feet, paws raised approximately eight feet in the air. The bear let out a growl that sounded like thunder rolling in his ears. Brice was terrified, paralyzed; he couldn't even breathe. The bear then roared out, stumbling slightly closer. Recalling what his dad had told him, he jumped up on a large rock beside him, threw his arms in the air, and lurched at the bear. As he swung his arms from side to side, he heard the truck keys in his pocket.

He jumped down from the rock and began to run toward the truck. As he darted, the bear followed. Brice pulled the keys from his pocket in mid-stride and squeezed the panic button to sound off the truck alarm. The bear stopped in its tracks. It stared curiously for a few seconds at the flashing lights and source of the loud beeps before vanishing back into the depths of the woods. Brice jumped in the truck and sped off, flinging dirt and gravel in the air behind him.

He drove just until he got to the mouth of the hollow and

pulled over to the side of the road. He powered up his cell phone and called 911, and frantically told the story. The operator's tone went from serious to shocked when she allowed, "Holy Shit!" to slip out. She apologized and told Brice to sit still. The police were on their way. She continued speaking more calmly, "Please turn the hazard light on the vehicle so the police can find you easily."

Back at the cave, Isis was doing all she knew how by keeping him warm by the fire and hydrated with her herbal tea. However, John had lost consciousness sometime around 3:00 pm. She was beginning to fear her family would find them before help could arrive. Her dad had split their search party in half with three men to each group. There was certainly a lot of mountain terrain to hunt, but Isis was also clever by covering their tracks as they went.

The cop car showed up about twenty to thirty minutes after Brice's call. Once they verified it was not a hoax, they called for backup and a search party. They explained that unless he could take them straight to his dad, they might have to wait until morning, as they were losing daylight. Not sure if he could, Brice told them it was no problem, afraid they would leave. They dispatched not only police backup but also an ambulance and a chopper. To make the search go more quickly, they even went door to door asking for anyone that had an ATV to relinquish it and/or help with the investigation. The neighbors jumped at the chance to help. Five ATVs and two side by sides headed into the woods with Brice and the police, as well as a medic.

It wasn't long before they all rolled up at the cave entrance. The men from the compound had gotten there just minutes prior and were inside the cave. Isis came running out and hugged Brice. She shouted in a loud panicked voice, "They're here!"

The police pulled their weapons and approached the cave. "Mason County P.D. Come out with your hands up!"

The men were placed under arrest and taken out two at

a time on the side by sides. Once the cave was clear, the medic entered and began working on John. He checked his vitals and began administering fluids through an I.V. The police arranged for transport via the chopper. They had to carry John to a clearing for them to airlift him out of the woods. Brice and Isis were taken back to the ambulance and transported to the hospital.

The National Guard was sent to capture the remaining persons within the compound, who were taken into custody. The children were placed in an already overcrowded foster care system. John's road to healing was long and painful, but he did eventually make a full recovery. Brice finally told the truth about his mom's boyfriend and elected to move in with his dad. John requested and was accepted to become a foster parent for Isis.

It wasn't long before the story hit the national news. Questions began to surface about whether a more effective vaccine could be developed by using the discovery of the compound family's approach, but in a humane way. Scientists and politicians are currently working on an ethical strategy for a new vaccine.

Chapter Four - The Dead

Mummies Are We?

I'm not sure of my story
Bits come and go
Life in the asylum
Is really all that I know

I do earnestly recall
How I did not fit in
I felt out of place
A dirty secret within

Days came not easy
Night terrors too long
Screams from the left room
From the right, she sang songs

Across the hall from my door
A giggling mess
Always drooling and peeing
And her hair a rat's nest

Soft music echoes
At the corridor's end
Children twirl and then speak
To make-believe friends

I'm hungry but can't eat

This slop they call food
My stomach launches it out
Airborne, like dust from a broom

I've become frail
I can feel my bones creak
My skin cracks and then bleeds
My time left is all bleak

Another night passes
I awake with the sun
My eyes cannot open
To me, what have they done?

I can't move my fingers
No whisper escapes
I don't think I'm breathing
No! No air I intake!

I feel cold and alone
Am I alive, did I pass?
No light to follow
No fire has been cast

I'm shuffled around
From a gurney to trunk
Then unto some table
Beside a jar of some gunk

My body is stripped
And fully inspected
My lids are pulled opened
I must be infected

I can now see
A workbench of the mad
Is that a hand in a jar
Oh my, this is bad

I force my eyes down
Run along the wood planks
There's a head on a shelf
Like a body-parts bank!

Quickly I shift
My eyes to the right
More horror awaits
In that terrible sight

An infant, a child
Laid down to rest
But its body is weird
It's shriveled, distressed

What is this place
I wonder in fear
As my eyes found a second

Human body lay near

A man then appears
Chatting success
My formula is perfect
Preservation in death

He mixed a concoction
Yielding some smoke
I fell into slumber
And never awoke

I feel different now
My presence so thin
When a breeze blows
It comes from within

A different view
From any angle I choose
I can see all
Hamrick and his muse

The hands on the clock
Race 'round so fast
Turned into liars
The sands of the glass

Graham Hamrick, our owner
Let us travel the world

With our new circus family
We were popular girls

Back home to Hamrick
In Philippi we stayed
Smithsonian placed bids
But he refused to be paid

Waters gushed in
And swallowed our home
Our bodies washed out
Onto the post office lawn

We were then laid out
Exposed to all eyes
To dry in the sun
And not even disguised

Hamrick had died
So the mortician in town
Tended to our bodies
Never wrapped nor bound

We were then lost
Many years had passed
Our baby disappeared
As did the head behind glass

Not sure who it was

The man, slept over me
But when he too died
Under his bed, I was freed

My companion in death
She was found in a barn
We were put on display
In reach of our arms

We've had many adventures
After our 1888 death
And our anonymity remains
As our names lost with our breath

Resting in glass boxes
We enjoy our sweet slumber
And our visitors marvel, as -
We are still Hamrick's grand thunder.

Ashes to Ashes

Just as Graham Hamrick and his mummies from Philippi, West Virginia, enjoyed dabbling in death, working to create a form of preservation of the dead, Jax and his brother discovered an alternative on what to do with the dead, one that was the complete opposite of what Hamrick did. Jax was born in 1968. He was raised by hippies addicted to sex and peace while dedicated to drugs and fighting the draft. Jax was not innocent to the smells of reefer and the view of the coffee table full of empty bottles of booze while stepping over passed-out adults to get ready for school.

During his young life, Jax became the primary caretaker of his baby brother, Jamison, born in 1973. He watched the rise and fall of his parents' lifestyle and realized their happiest moments were when they were both submissive to an incredible high. However, he also observed the consequences of it all, even in their days of sobriety and recovery. He bore witness to his mother, Gretchen, and her grief through one miscarriage in 1974 and then a forced abortion by his father in 1975. His father, Ben, had accused her of being with other men and refused to support a bastard child, despite her constant claims the baby was his. Maybe it was the booze or the drugs that clouded Ben's judgment but looking back now, Jax believed his mom was telling the truth.

Jax remembered another life-changing event like it was yesterday. He watched his father grab his thin-framed mother by the throat, holding her against the wall. As he allowed her to slide slowly back down to her feet, he grabbed her by her long blond hair and dragged her to the bedroom. As Jax peeked around the corner, he saw his dad throw her on the bed while yelling, "I am your husband! Tonight, you will screw me!" He then backhanded her across the face, bringing blood to her upper lip. After climbing off her for a moment, he slammed the door in Jax's face.

Though afraid for his mother's safety, as well as for Jamison and himself, Jax's anger began to erupt as he listened to his mother's cries. Despite the lack of bonding, parental care, and attention, Jax still loved his mother and felt a duty to protect her and Jamison.

He slowly opened the door to the second bedroom, painted dark blue with the solar system glowing on the ceiling. He saw his twin-sized bed dressed with an ugly, thin, worn, brown blanket just adjacent to an old, wood crib, with white paint peeling off, all immediately across the hall from his parents' room. Jax was ensuring his brother was still asleep and safe.

He then slipped into the living room, grabbing the phone and dragging the long cream-colored cord, just barely reaching inside the hall closet. As he hid behind the closet door, Jax called 911. He whispered into the pea-green handset, "Please, send help, my Mommy is being hurt!"

Jax laid the phone down inside the closet while the operator was still speaking and crawled quietly to his parents' door. Still on his knees, he leaned over and placed his ear against the door. He could hear his mother crying with an occasional thump. He then crawled back across the hall to his bedroom, where his baby brother slept.

Jax heard the sirens, followed by blue lights flashing into the windows. The commotion between Ben and Gretchen, along with the pounding on the front door, awoke Jamison. Jax ran to the door to let the police in; as they entered, he turned to run back to his crying brother. By this time, Ben had pulled up his pants and met Jax in the hall. He yelled, "What have you done now? You spoiled little shit!" Jax managed to get past his father as the police moved in and cuffed Ben.

Once in custody, fingerprinted, and DNA samples collected, Ben was moved from the holding cell at the precinct to the county jail, following his arraignment. While locked up in county, the SVU (Special Victims Unit) detectives matched his DNA and fingerprints to three previous rape cases over the past six years. Ben was found guilty of domestic battery, child endangerment, and four counts of assault and rape. He was sentenced to 15 years with a minimum of ten years served in prison before being eligible for parole.

As Jax grew from scrawny bones and skin into a masculine, dark physique, he made it his life's mission to find the middle ground, where one could indulge in the rush of a fantasy world without the costly consequence to follow. Meanwhile, as the days passed into years, Gretchen quit visiting Ben in prison yet went back to school seeking a bachelor's degree in Criminal Justice. Through the long nights of studying, tests, and papers, Jax and even young Jamison had to take up the slack, watching their mother better herself. Jax realized the importance of an education as he watched his mother struggle between boyfriends and bills.

Jax, excelling through school while trying to uplift and encourage Jamison, tangled in a constant wrestling match of right and wrong. He was trying to keep Jamison out of trouble. All of the stress had created a giant ball of emotions like a hard-knotted rock in the middle of his stomach. Meanwhile, he had to deal with his own high level of stress and the blame game of life's woes. He was trying to understand and make sense of the sporadic racing blood pressure and chest pains that the doctors had no explanation for, which only added to the ghostly disease infecting and incapacitating his youthful body. Yet he pushed on as he realized he was the man of the house now.

In 1991, Ben, still fat but older and balder, was released from prison, and as he slipped away from their memories, he seemed to disappear publicly. He changed his name from Benjamin Patrick Casto to Michael Benjamin Caid and moved out of state. Despite crossing the state line and settling down in a small town in Tennessee, Mike Caid stayed close enough to his now ex-wife and two sons to maintain his obsession and watchful eye.

He was not ready to give up control, especially seeing as they were the reason he had just spent a chunk of his life in the pen.

Gretchen had begun a romance with one of her professors. It was a short six-month affair that ended just before she graduated. Yet, she split on good terms with the professor, who even assisted Gretchen in acquiring a position as an insurance fraud investigator. Not officially on the police force, ironically, she worked closely with the homicide department on cases involving questionable life insurance claims. This would soon bring her face to face with the old Ben disguised as Mike Caid of Caid Crematory and Mortuary.

While in prison, Mike had made some very shady but equally influential and wealthy friends. His new partners fully funded his new business dealing with the dead with the understanding that he would repay through human disposal acts when called upon. Mike found himself cremating noncompliant bodies for the Mob. He was living large and spared no expense to keep his family in check. Once in a while, he would have them followed. Occasionally, he hired someone to step in to influence their decisions. Whether it be paying someone off to not hire them for a job, or someone selling them something they needed, dirt cheap. Truth be told, he was probably the cause of Gretchen's new failed love with the criminal justice professor, maybe through bribes or threats. Not actually being an officer or agent himself, but a mere civilian, the professor would probably do the sensible thing and just end the said relationship.

Mike wasn't entirely ignorant, though; he knew his place and stayed in it. He never dabbled in nor spoke of the Mob's business. He simply did the deeds when he was called upon and left it at that. So, when Gretchen showed up sitting in her car with a camera in hand in front of his establishment, he didn't approach her. He did, however, follow her until she reached a place he felt was somewhat safe and out of the surveillance zones of the Mob. She stayed at what many would call a fleabag motel; apparently, investigative work didn't reimburse much for expenses. He watched from the parking lot, under the sign flashing vacancies, as she made her way to room 202. He thought that was smart; she *got a room on the second level to overlook the lot yet still close to the exit.* He was confident she had no clue what she just stepped into, and he hoped she at least had a gun.

Mike decided to let it be. She only took a few pics of the exterior front of the Crematory during downtime. She couldn't have gotten anything incriminating. Returning to his desk, at his place of business, he couldn't help but worry over Gretchen's safety. Then the phone rang. "Hello?" Mike answered.

"So, your little woman is sticking her nose where it doesn't belong. You have 24 hours to snuff this, or we snuff her. And, you will have a delivery at midnight," the voice stated.

Mike pleaded in surprise, "Wait! She's just an insurance agent. She has no clue what's going on. Trust me; she's too stupid to put anything together!" The call was immediately disconnected.

Mike drove back to the motel where Gretchen was staying. He went to her room and knocked, but there was no answer. He inquired at the front desk of her whereabouts, and the clerk informed him that she had just gone to the diner across the street. Although he was still harboring ill thoughts toward her, he still didn't want to see her murdered. She was his baby's momma, after all. He stood on the street corner for a spell, watching her through the giant transparent windows. As her food arrived, he was reassured she was eating alone and decided to join her.

He slid into the booth across from her at the same table. She choked on her drink when she realized who he was. "What the hell are you doing here?" she gasped.

"Gretchen, the real question is, what the hell are you doing here? You have no idea who you are screwing with. You need to pack up and go back home to the boys immediately." He spoke softly but with great urgency.

She snapped back, "You're the one that needs to leave. I got a restraining order against you when I heard you were released. As far as my boys, they are grown men now and living their own lives."

Mike let out a little bit of a laugh; then, his face was wiped down into a solemn glare. "I know about the boys; I've been watching you all. I know how you screwed up Jamison, how he is a useless drug addict now. I also know how despite the college degree that Jax has got, he is still struggling to make ends meet. I know how you screwed your professor and the lives of our boys. But what you don't know is the danger you just tangled yourself up in."

She motioned for the waitress and asked for a to-go box and the check. "I am a licensed private investigator, and I know exactly what I am doing."

"No, you are an insurance claims investigator, and you have no idea what you are doing, or even who you are doing. The Caid Crematory and Mortuary is owned and operated by me. My name is now Mike Caid and what you are investigating is not worth a $50,000 insurance compliance suit. You have just stepped into the back-alley dealings of the Mob. Get your ass out of town and tell your boss you found nothing here."

Gretchen paid her bill, boxed up her food, and as she threw a tip on the table, said, "The cash is for the waitress. My tip to you is to leave me the hell alone, or you will find yourself back in jail." She then walked out of the diner and went back to the hotel. Settling into her room, she sat on the bed and opened her to-go box with her dinner. She, however, could not quit dwelling on his words that 'she had just stepped into the business of the Mob.' If that's the case, then he was right. Although she had gone through standardized self-defense training, required by law for her private investigation license, she had not completed any police training.

She took a few bites of her club sandwich but seemed to

have lost her appetite. She decided to call Paul, her ex-boyfriend and professor. He seemed quite happy to hear from her until she began explaining what had just happened. Paul quickly replied, "Gretchen, babe. You know I am also a judge, not just a professor, so I cannot give any legal advice. As a friend, I'd say drop the case and get back home ASAP." His sharp tone made it clear that something was indeed wrong about the whole situation. After they said goodbye, she opened her laptop and created an email to her boss. She was planning on resigning from this particular assignment and holding off for the next job.

Meanwhile, Mike had returned to the crematory to receive his next client. As promised, the delivery was made right at midnight, through the garage attached to the back of the building. As he unloaded the body onto a gurney for transport into the basement, he suddenly felt the cold hard end of a revolver on his temple. "This is your last chance. You have already been warned. Now we will be taking care of the little woman. From this moment on, you will forget she ever existed. If you pursue this, you can share a chamber with her in your furnace." Mike nodded in understanding and continued to move the Mob's victim inside and into the furnace room.

The next day, Mike, concerned for Gretchen, went back to the hotel. He had to convince her to give this up and go back home to their sons. However, when he got there, the door to her motel room was slightly ajar. He pushed it open with his sleeve, already suspecting foul play. There was no sign of Gretchen. It appeared as if all of her belongings were still there, including her laptop perched on top of the bed beside last night's uneaten dinner. Dried blood had crusted over the corner and halfway across the screen and keyboard. There were three chunks of human debris on the keyboard entangled with a few hairs. Mike fell to his knees, eye-level with the laptop on the bed. The matter left behind had very few tinges of white or cream-colored like one would anticipate seeing in a horror movie. Instead, it was primarily black and grey pieces of what looked like tissue trying to escape through the dark dried blood.

He began to gag at the sight and realized he needed to get out of that room before he was seen or unexpectedly left incriminating evidence, such as vomit. He quickly exited the room, pulled the door back as he found it with his jacket sleeve, and left the motel. He went back to the crematory but couldn't shake what he had just seen. *Where did they take her body, he wondered? Why would they take her body and leave so much evidence behind? It just didn't make sense.* The phone rang, and Mike answered, "Hello?"

The voice replied, "You have another delivery. The package will arrive in twenty minutes. Don't screw this up, or you're next."

No. They wouldn't be so heartless, so cold! They wouldn't bring her body to me! What am I thinking? Of course, they would. This is the damn Mob run by Stefano Garcia, who no doubt was about to teach me a lesson in Mob-related ethics and loyalty!

The delivery arrived. Mike didn't look at the body; he already knew it was Gretchen. He loaded the corpse onto the gurney, business as usual. One of the large men explained, "Stefano expects the same service as usual. Any funny business, and you're next. It's too late for her anyway. Just get on with it."

Without even looking up from Gretchen's fresh corpse, wrapped in a blood-soaked white sheet, he muttered, "Yes, of course! Business as usual." Then wheeled her body into the furnace room for disposal as they left.

As he rolled her body through the slumber room to the elevator, he couldn't help but reach down and take her shoulder into his hand. He could tell from the wrapped sheet around her that most of her head was gone. He began to shed a few tears while pushing her into the furnace room in the basement. He fired up the furnace, then began to prepare the cremation casket, which is simply a cardboard box in the shape of an old pauper's coffin. It was positioned on another gurney that sat much lower than the first. This made for easy transfer from one to the next with the least amount of contact with the corpse. One person could easily roll the body into the box alone.

Mike had done this a thousand times or more with no issues. But he had never cremated someone he had loved before either. He had to, he just had to look. Something kept telling him that he just had to make sure it was her. He pulled the sheet back. His suspicions were correct. She was missing too much of her face to identify her positively. Yet, he recalled the little peace sign tattoo on her right breast. So, he pulled the sheet down further. It was there! Yes, it was her; undeniably, it was her. He quickly covered her back up and shoved her body into the flaming furnace.

He collected her ashes as he had always done with his legit clients, but in the most beautiful urn. He went as far as to have the in-house tech engrave a 24k gold tag to be affixed to it. He sat quietly in his office. He was recounting every detail of their screwed-up lives and all of the mistakes he had made. He decided he had to make this right, somehow. He turned on the computer and constructed his will. In the said document, he was leaving everything to be equally divided between their two sons, Jax and Jamison, including Caid's Crematory and Mortuary. Mike knew his days were already numbered, so he also sat down and wrote a letter to the police. He confessed his sins, describing in detail his part in the illegal activity of the Mob. He selected cc on the email to include the local papers, and then he hit send.

Grabbing the hidden bottle of Grand Marnier from his desk, he drove down to the levee. He cranked up a little CCR, opened his car doors, and walked over to the river bank. Mike pulled out his cell, and in a group message typed:

Boys, I am so sorry for all the pain I have caused you. Your mother got messed up with the Mob on this last assignment she was on. I know bc I was a part of it. They murdered her in her motel. I wish I could change things. I wish I could bring her back. I'm sorry I sucked as a dad. But I do love you both. I have done well since prison and am leaving you boys everything. Please make better choices than I did, and be sure the ones you love know it. I'm so sorry, Dad.

Determined to leave this world on his terms, he placed a Glock between his teeth and fired.

Caid's Crematory and Mortuary was turned over to the young men but remained under investigation for months. Jax and Jamison took over their father's establishment. Despite conflicts between them, they had been busy fulfilling previous set contracts that Mike already had on the books. The two fought over if they would keep the prosperous business or sell it. Jamison liked the idea of easy work for big paydays, but Jax knew the company had been contaminated with illegal and unethical deals. Besides, Jax didn't want anything from the man that had not only caused them so much pain but ultimately admitted to partial responsibility for their mother's death.

They were eventually permitted to cremate their father's corpse. That event didn't go as well as expected. Jamison's solid, defined muscular body had been relaxed on the couch of the slumber room, where private visitation and identification took place, as well as the waiting room for clients when the furnace room was packed. He had taken maybe a line or two too many of the synthetic coke he had been accustomed to. This significantly differed from the visitation aka observation room where families gathered to say their goodbyes to the deceased. Jax, running his hand through his thick, dark blond hair, had been sorting through the financial records in the office, uncovering many discrepancies and heightening his awareness of illegal operations and funding.

When the two finally came together to accept and transport Mike, their father's body, to the furnace room, all hell broke loose. Jax told his brother that Mike had been dealing in some shady shit, and they needed to just unload the business on someone else and get out. Jamison, downright belligerent, said he would not give up his dad's business.

Jax yelled at Jamison, "This was not built for us by a father! Dammit, he never gave us anything in life! He was a damn criminal and crook! He was never a dad!"

Jamison replied with as much passion as he could muster in his red face, "Exactly! Which is why we deserve this!" He smiled and rubbed his nose, "Besides, he was the only dad I knew, and he left us a profitable business."

Jax, even more angrily, yelled, "Jamison, he was screwing around with the Mob! That's why he and Mom are dead! We need to sell this shit and get back home."

As they stood in the elevator going down to the basement, Jamison's nose began to bleed. He smeared the blood across his upper lip and left cheek then said, "Bro, you can do whatever you want, but I'm staying in! We aren't him, and I'm betting since the cops have been all over this joint, the Mob is done with it. This is easy money!"

The elevator stopped at the basement, and they wheeled their father's body out and into the furnace room. As Jax grabbed the gurney with the cardboard crypt, he told Jamison to ensure the ashtray had been emptied from the previous burn. Jamison laughed as he pulled the empty tray and announced, "Clear to proceed, Captain!"

Jax, annoyed at his brother's response, had already rolled the body into the cardboard casket. "Should we look?" he asked.

"Why not?" Jamison replied with a smirk and shrug of the shoulders. They unzipped the bag that the FBI had provided. The facial features were null from the bullet's disbursement, as well as the swelling and decay of the corpse. Jax quickly zipped the bag closed and shoved the body in the fiery furnace.

Once the light turned green, Jamison pulled the tray of ashes out. "So, now what?" he asked.

Jax merely replied, "I say we just dump them in the trash."

Being the reasonable one for the first time, Jamison spoke up and said, "Yeah, well, he was infected. Right?"

Jax, completely dumbfounded, spoke with great curiosity, "What?"

Jamison continued as he held up the FBI folder containing the autopsy report. "Umm, yeah, Bro, legally we can't just dump him, and you want to be Mr. Right. This report says that he had been infected with this damn virus that is killing people. If you dump dad's ashes, you are the primary cause of this pandemic's continual spread and become an enemy of the state. You will become enemy number one, a terrorist and traitor."

Jax stumbled back against the wall in complete disbelief of his luck. Jamison continued to taunt and tease, "Hey Bro, the Mr. Goodie two-shoes act ends here! Find your balls, and man up! What you gonna do now? Hey, I have an idea! Let's snort him!"

Jamison laughed as he grabbed his brother and tried to force his face into their father's tray of ashes. A few punches were thrown, a couple of failed attempts of a sleeper hold until Jamison finally shoved Jax's face in the tray of ashes. "This place is our out! This is our break! You won't screw this up for me!" he yelled as he tried to suffocate Jax in Mike's remains.

Jax subsequently inhaled the ashes of his infected, suicidal father. As he did so, Jamison yelled, "I am not going back to rehab! I am not going back on the streets! This is my out, and you will not screw it up!" Jax slid out of his arms like a melting icicle onto the floor. Mere seconds passed when Jax sat up and was talking about angels and rainbows. It was as if he had just received the Holy Ghost, wholly filled with peace, love, and all that felt good. Jax grabbed hold of Jamison, using his jacket as a means of a ladder to pull himself back up to his feet.

"Damn!" Jax said. "Dude! You have to try it!"

Jamison started laughing, "You stupid shit! That's a dead

body, not coke! You can't get high off the dead!" Jax grabbed the back of Jamison's head and shoved his face into the ashes. Without choice, Jamison took a deep breath sucking their father's ashes in, then slid to the floor out of Jax's grasp.

"Holy shit!" Jamison yelled out. "This is way better than any coke I've ever had! I wonder if dad is as addictive; he sure as hell is a better high!" The two sat back down on the cold, hard floor of the furnace room, each escaping reality to become fully immersed in a fantasy world of never-ending colors, peace, and euphoria.

"Hey, Jamison. You remember that guy Hamrick that I did my West Virginia studies project on, back in school?"

Jamison laughing hysterically, "You mean that dude that mummified women from the insane asylum? Yeah, he was a freak!"

Jax shoved his brother over while sitting against the concrete wall beside him, "Yeah, him. You know, maybe he would have achieved his fame if he had just burned and snorted them bodies instead." The two began laughing like hyenas on crack.

Several hours later, when they woke from their high and crash, neither felt any repercussions. Neither had headaches, upset stomachs, shakes, not one typical hangover or side effect. Jax looked over to Jamison and said, "Dude, maybe we should keep this place. As far as I know, there are no laws against snorting the dead." Jamison began laughing.

They bagged up the remainder of their father's ashes, which came to nearly six pounds. They leveled it off right at the six-pound mark and divided the remaining ashes between the two of them for their personal use. Being a bit more informed on street drugs than Jax, Jamison explained that a typical 8 ball of coke runs around $1100 to $1200. "Well, how much is an 8-ball?" Jax asked. Jamison explained it was approximately 8 grams.

"Damn!" Jax replied, Pop's ashes are right at 6 pounds, that means … hmmm let me think, there are about 454 grams per pound, divided by 8 grams …." Jax looked up at Jamison in awe and continued, "Damn! That's like 57 8-balls from just one pound! Multiply that by 6 … is hmmm … like 340 8-balls!"

Jamison smiled from ear to ear and replied, "Yeah, Bro, and 340 8 balls will bring in over 400,000 dollars! And that's just off of dad!"

Jax sighed. He knew this wasn't right, and somehow, someway, he knew it would be illegal. "But I'm not a drug dealer! I don't even use drugs! I saw the aftermath of what drugs can do, from watching Mom and Pops!"

Jamison grabbed his brother's shoulders, "But that's the thing, Bro! Technically, this isn't even drugs! Yet, it gives a way better high without all of the side effects! Who knows, we may even bust open the scientific field with this, as a cure for addictions!"

Jax spoke up, "Yeah, okay, whatever, but who is going to sell it?" Jamison smiled again; "I'll take care of that. You just burn 'em and bag 'em!"

A few weeks passed, and Jamison was getting complaints that the product quality was diminishing. It just wasn't delivering the same intense buzz it had before. Jamison and Jax quickly realized that the only corpses that could be effectively converted into what they called the zombie rush, Z-Rush, or ZR for short, were from the bodies that had been infected with the virus.

Jax, always a bit of a prude, said, "So, it's not working with normal corpses, and I can't keep from wondering if we're spreading the virus more by using the infected? Besides, someone is eventually going to notice that the ashes of their loved ones are a bit thin."

Jamison argued, "No, because those that used the ZR drug created by the infected seemed to become immune. It may actually be a natural cure, a vaccine. If you recall, when we started distributing pop's ashes, the numbers seemed to drop here locally. Jax, I'm telling you, not only have we found the cure for the opioid and heroin addictions, we found the cure for the freaking pandemic!"

Jax replied with a sigh, "Maybe, but we can never tell anyone, so it is still useless."

It wasn't long before Stefano Garcia's goons started circling again, like sharks hunting prey. They had been watching and waiting to make their move in reestablishing a new contract with Mike's sons and their crematory. They had been monitoring their every movement, from daily business to personal purchases and lifestyles. Stefano wasn't stupid. You can't buy fancy sports cars, move into the Upper Side, and entertain the wealthy on a typical income from a crematory.

Now that evidence was indeed surfacing that what was going on had to be more than just funerals and cremations, Stefano wanted his cut. It was his building and investment anyway. That building, that business, were both fully funded by him, and therefore those young men and their new enterprise belonged to him as well. Stefano sent his thugs to the Caid Crematory to investigate. He wanted to know how these two young men were acquiring such large incomes from such a small-town business of death.

Romero, a hired hand of Stefano, and his crew burst into the crematory, demanding all of the books. Simultaneously, one of the smaller men bedecked in a cheesy 1990s windbreaker grabbed up all of the accounting books. He clinched them tight against his chest and backed himself into a corner. Romero forced Jax by gunpoint to open the safe, yet was dismayed by the hollow shell that stood before them. His anger was amplified by his memories as a child when he opened that Easter egg that he was so proud to find, only it held no candy. He slammed Jax against the wall, "Stefano wants to know where you are getting your money!" His sizable hairy forearm smashed Jax's face into the drywall.

"What money?" Jax muttered from his smushed mouth.

"Don't play dumb, asshole! Stefano knows all about your big houses and fancy cars," Romero growled.

As Jax began to talk, Romero let him loose just a little. "Are you serious? That shit was paid for from our mom's insurance policy! She was an insurance investigator and was killed while on an assignment. That was an automatic accidental death claim in addition to worker's comp death, and she had regular life insurance. I hate to say it, God rest her soul, but my brother and I made out quite well by her death because of her insight. We didn't even need or want this damn place!"

Romero let Jax go but replied, "You ungrateful, cold-hearted prick! You don't deserve a dime." He raised his gun and clocked Jax in the head, knocking him unconscious. As Jax lay on the floor, the other two thugs trashed the office looking for additional books and money.

Jamison walked in on the mayhem that was going down and saw his brother on the floor. Not knowing whether he was alive or dead, he looked from corner to corner of the room with everything tossed sideways and upside down. His temper high on the ZR drug, he reacted before thinking, and pulled out a gun. "Who the hell are you? What have you done?"

Romero pointed his gun at Jamison. "Don't do anything stupid, son."

"I don't know who you are, and I sure as hell am not your son!" Jamison shouted as he directed his revolver toward Romero. He looked down to his brother, Jax, lying on the floor, believing in his heart he was dead, and blamed himself. He looked back up full of guilt and anger into Romero's eyes and hissed, "You can tell your fat-ass boss, now he will never know the ingredients of the best drug ever made. But more importantly, let him know the cure for this virus and true fame that would have come with it just slipped out of his hands!" Jamison fired three rounds into Romero's chest, moments before one of the tall thugs, dressed all in black, who had been standing in the corner behind him, stepped up, placed his gun against the back of his head, and fired. Jamison's scalp, face, hair, and brain matter blew all over the room.

Those remaining of Stefano's crew took the books and walked away, leaving Romero's body lying in the office along with what was left of Jamison and the unconscious Jax.

Two weeks later, Jax awoke in a hospital from a coma, experiencing short-term memory loss. He kept asking for his mother and brother. The nurses tried to be as patient as possible while repeatedly explaining to him that they had both passed away. Through the next few days, Jax began to get fragments of flashes of his life that were all jumbled up like dreams. He wasn't sure if the flashback of his abusive father was real. Did he and his brother really find the cure for the new plague? Were the visions of him and his brother burning their father's body and snorting his ashes just a freakish nightmare? … it had to be … he would never do something so vile.

Chapter Five – Victim

Charlie

There once was a girl named Charlie

Who never said I'm sorry

For a neck with a crook

Revenge she took

And his spike is now pushing up barley

Doug

I sat at the end of the short bar and ordered up another Jack and Coke. At 2:00 PM there was no crowd, only three other customers in the whole place. An older woman with short, white hair sinking money into the video lottery machines and two other older men sitting on the patio with a beer. The bartender had the news on the TV while playing music from his phone over the karaoke speakers. He sat my drink down on the bar in front of me, collected my $6.50 and empty glass, then walked back to pick up his phone. He wasn't much of a sociable, friendly kind of guy, reflected by my paltry tips. I suppose one could say the lack of tip actually initiated his lack of serving and social skills. It doesn't matter when it's simply one asshole serving another.

One of the older men from the patio came over to the bar to get another beer. He stood freakishly close to me. Not only did my homophobic-anger radar kick in, but the fact that he was not obeying the social distancing, mask-wearing, space-respecting rules of this new world plague pissed me off. I pushed him away from me, giving him a what-the-fuck look, grabbed my drink, and shoulder bumped him as I went out on the patio. The bartender, still with his nose to his phone, pretended to have no clue as to what had happened. I could see him through the door, giving the guy another beer.

I lit up a cigar and sat down beside the fire pit. As I looked over to the tall table where I met Mazy, I recall her beautiful long, blond hair hanging down, slightly covering her cleavage. I smiled, remembering how she smelled of coconuts and vanilla, how her skin tasted on my tongue. It was sad that she was so feisty; maybe she would have lasted longer. She reminded me of a good piece of apple pie a-la-mode. Warm and creamy, yet the joys of her flavor in my mouth vanished too quickly. I finished my drink, and smoke, then went back inside the bar. By this time, that guy had already chugged down his last beer and left.

I decided to sit back down and get one more before hitting the road. Maybe a different flavor would stop in before I left. I paid for one more when the news ticker across the bottom of the screen caught my eye. Mazy Reynolds, age 23, still missing from Putnam County. Meanwhile, the details of a new report flashed on the full screen regarding discoveries about this virus. It was a bullet list:

- People with blood type O - are less susceptible to contracting the virus
- The virus has now been found to mutate with each person it affects
- Due to recent findings of these mutations, vaccines are not working
- Scientists are finding DNA samples attached to strands of the virus
- Contact Tracing is predicted to go from phone calls to DNA testing

Well, that can't be good, I thought. This possibly means no cure to this airborne contagion that has been killing people for the last year. I became a little nervous and decided to go back home to do some cleaning. I needed to step up my game. After all, an ounce of prevention is worth avoiding 20 years behind bars. I finished my drink and left.

Once I got home, I rolled the large area rug out of the loft onto the barn's main floor. I was cautious grabbing the ropes, blanket, towel, dog collar, and dog bowls, as well as the plastic bucket. I rolled all items that she may have touched, ate off of, and puked, peed, and pooped on inside the rug. I pulled the rolled-up rug and incriminating evidence inside it down by the creek, positioning it within the already charred circle where I burn the trash because I refuse to pay $67 per month for people to come to get trash! Dousing it with gasoline, I lit it up like the Fourth of July. The smell of pee and poop on fire damn near knocked me over. The stench was awful, so I decided to go back to the house where I could still watch the fire but also the TV at the same time.

I popped open a beer, grabbed a bag of sour cream chips, and settled down into my recliner. Just as I was beginning to relax, my phone rang. You know that annoying ringtone when someone is trying to call you through a video app. I spilled my freaking beer while trying to get it out of my pocket, but by that time it had already quit. Then a text popped up.

Hey dude, you burning trash again?

The smoke is rolling black up this side of the hill.

It was Jason; most likely, his nosey girlfriend made him ask me. That woman has her chains on him and wears the pants in that household. I replied with a quick,

Yeah, no worries, it's under control.

Days turned into a week or more, and I became so bored and lonely sitting in this stupid trailer by myself. Staring at the deer head on the wall, I couldn't quit thinking about Dad. Although I had lost bits and pieces of those memories over the years, there was one that I could not shake off—a haunting type that seems to be a nightmare on repeat. Anyway, to top it off, every time the wind would blow, the damn antenna would spin around, wiping out all but one channel on the TV. Can't get the internet out here. I'm lucky just to get a half bar on this piece of crap cell phone and have to be sitting in the recliner to get that. I guess that's only because it's right beside the big bay window. Now, that's funny, who pays to put a big bay window in a single-wide mobile home but doesn't invest in drywall and insulation? Dad, that's who.

I walked outside to get a few more logs to throw in the wood burner, saw my truck, and thought to myself, what the hell? I need more beer anyway. I grabbed my keys and headed into town. After running into the store for beer and microwave dinners, I drove over to *Langley's Long-Horn*. Maybe I wasn't the only one tired of being in quarantine. I walked in and ordered a shot of whiskey and a beer. I downed the shot, grabbed my beer, and walked out on the patio. I sat down at the table and listened to the latest drunken gossip of who went home with who, as those young idiots winked and punched each other in the arms.

A young man walked out carrying a drink and sat at the table across from me. He pulled out a bowl of weed, lit a bit, hit it then offered it to me. I shook my head, declining. He nodded, took another hit, snuffed it with his thumb, then slipped it back in his coat pocket. I began to get nervous because I realized I had been oddly staring at him. The resemblance was uncanny! With his long, dirty blond hair and a three-day beard, he could have been Chris's twin. That sent my mind whirling around again on rewind, back to that nightmarish memory.

Dad would take me and my brother, Chris, hunting on top of the mountain behind the trailer. Extremely close to where Jason lives now. While walking up the hill that day, Chris was bragging about stealing Amy's virginity. He was very detailed about how being forceful with her seemed to turn her on as much as it did him. Dad became so angry he punched Chris in the face, knocking him on his ass. "We don't take anything! Especially from a woman!" Dad screamed at him, then took off ahead of us to the tiny cabin he had at the top of the hill. When the two of us finally caught up with him, he had already broken into and sucked down half a bottle of rum.

The young man asked me if I had heard the latest news on that missing girl, snapping me out of my memory bank of horrors. I shook my head no, and he proceeded to share. "I dated her for about two months, I guess I dodged that bullet. They are saying that during the investigation, the police found unheard voicemails and unread emails, stating that she had been exposed to the virus and needed to get tested and go into quarantine ASAP. So, she was walking around infected, probably spreading that shit, to who knows how many men."

Taken by surprise, all I could say was, "Wow." All along,

I was thinking to myself, that means I'm probably infected too. Dammit!

I walked back inside and ordered a double shot. My mind raced between the recent memories of Mazy and memories of my dad and Chris. One minute I saw her long pretty hair twisted with the hay from the barn and the next, my dad sitting on that makeshift log bed in the tiny run-down cabin, drinking rum. It felt like I was just listening to two different people in my head telling two different stories. Some parts seemed to overlap other details, making it difficult to discern between the two incidents.

I found myself ordering another double when I saw my new flavor at the other end of the bar. She was sitting in one of the tall leather back chairs. She twisted from one side to the other as different men tried to keep her engaged in conversation while buying her drinks. At one time or another, she had caught the attention of every man in that joint but had me mesmerized. Her dark-red hair made her bright, green eyes pop out like a grassy field during a beautiful red sunset. I could get so lost in her sweet floral fragrance forever. I waited while watching her every move.

She picked up her drink and made her way out to the patio for a smoke. As soon as she had placed the cigarette between her soft pink lips, I was there with a light. With each giggle and flick of her hair, I became more entranced. "What's your name, beautiful?" I asked.

She grinned and softly spoke, "I'm Grace Lynn."

Of course, she is, I thought. "Well, *Graceland*, I'm Doug." Confident in the big smile she just flashed in response, she was clearly interested. When her cup came close to being empty, I rushed in to get her another drink. I had to stay one step ahead of all the others. I managed to hold her attention most of the night, listening to all she had to say. Eventually, she asked about me.

It was literally like I had just crashed into a brick wall doing eighty. I gasped. The only thing I could think of was that cabin on the hill, my dad and my brother. "Well, I'm trying to drink away a memory tonight," I said, hoping she would let it go at that, but no, that just made me more attractive to her.

"A woman?" she asked.

"No, not at all; my heart has been shut down way longer than most of the business establishments during this pandemic." I smiled as she giggled at my response.

She continued to prod me for more information as she leaned flirtatiously closer. "Do tell," she whispered in my ear. I explained it was just too painful a story and maybe another time.

I backed off a little from the conversation as each man took his shot at winning her focus. I enjoyed watching her work the entire bar with her majestic powers and grinned when she cleverly shot down one man after another. She had been so admired; she never paid for one drink. As the night progressed, it became clear her friends got bored and left her. She had become completely intoxicated and was arguing on the phone with someone. I followed her out the door as the bar closed and, of course, offered her a ride home.

She accepted my offer, and I helped her into the car; as I did, she reminded me that I never told her what was bothering me. I couldn't resist her charm. I told her I would tell her on the way. We had no more than pulled out of the parking lot onto the main road when she announced with great urgency that she had to pee. I explained to her that the bar had already locked the doors, and there wasn't anything else open at 3:00 AM. Yet, I then got the best idea! "Wait, I know a place I can take you." Just a few blocks up the road was a turn-off that led out onto an old country backroad. I had been there before. I took Mazy there that night.

"Where are you taking me?" she asked.

"Well, you said you had to pee like right now, and everything is closed," I explained.

"But that gas station we just passed was open," she argued. Ignoring her comment, I kept driving.

I eventually pulled off the side of the road, where the area was large enough for about three cars if pulled straight on facing the cliffside. I helped her out of the car and handed her some napkins from the glovebox. I watched with a bit of a grin as she stumbled her way over to the large oak tree. I leaned against the car and lit a cigar, watching her slowly pull her shorts and panties down. Then she fell against the broad tree trunk.

"You need any help?" I asked in delight, catching a glimpse of her open legs.

"I'm good!" she yelled as if I had been sitting inside the car. When she was finished, I helped her back to the car. I stopped, opened the trunk on the way around to the driver's seat, and pulled out a bottle of hot cinnamon whiskey.

I climbed back inside the car, opened the bottle, handed it to her, brushed the hair back from her face, and kissed her cheek. She began to cry, pouring her heart out to me, telling me of the fight she had with her boyfriend earlier that night. I grabbed the bottle, took a swig, and gave it back to her, encouraging her to drink up.

"You do have amazing eyes. You are so beautiful. No man should ever ignore or mistreat you. I can see the pain in your eyes, and I feel like we are kindred souls." I laid my hand on her knee.

"So, are you going to tell me your story or not?" she asked as she gulped the bottle.

The next thing I knew, I heard myself telling her the story, picking up where my mind had left me, back at the bar.

"So, Dad was so angry at Chris, for basically admitting to raping Amy, who had lived just down the road with her older brother and unwed mom. We both knew what Chris had done was wrong but didn't realize just how bad it was."

Curiously she interrupted, "How so?"

I continued, "After the bottle of rum was gone, we followed Dad out behind the cabin. He had some beer stashed down in the old well to keep it cool."

She interrupted again, "That's actually a great idea."

I smiled, then proceeded with the story. "After he pulled the beer up from the well, he opened one, chugged it, then opened another. He did eventually offer me and Chris one. But then he said he had something to show us. Dad began to stagger around the cabin. Once we got to the other side, he opened the dilapidated old firewood box, and there was Amy. Only, it wasn't all of Amy."

She began to laugh, "Aw, you're shitting me!"

I slid my hand up her leg a little further and worked up a tear or two. "No, baby, for reals." I sighed. "My dad told us that Amy's brother brought her to our trailer, screaming some nonsense that we had raped her and now we all had to pay. He told her brother he didn't know anything about what had been done. He said he was going to call us to come home to get to the bottom of it, but Amy's brother pulled a gun out of his truck. Dad said he wasn't going to just stand there and let him shoot him, especially because he didn't even know what was going on."

I had her distracted by the story; she was following along so intensely. I watched her take a couple more drinks. Her pretty pink lips wrapping around the mouth of that bottle began to excite me.

She reached over and put her hand on my leg. "What happened?" she eagerly asked.

I put my other arm around her shoulder and pulled her a little closer, then continued. "Dad said he reached inside the door of the trailer and grabbed his shotgun off the wall."

At this point, I was looking directly down Graceland's blouse. I had to readjust myself. I took the bottle, got a drink, handed it back, then continued. "Dad said he cocked, pointed, then shot. He killed him. Of course, Amy, who was still sitting in the truck, jumped out and ran up the hill. Dad had to chase her and put her down too since she was a witness to her brother's death."

I told Grace how Dad said he burned her brother's body and raked what was left into the creek bed. He figured the water would do the rest. Amy was closer to the cabin when he shot her, so he decided to just hack her up with the ax. He had been burning her piece by piece in the cabin with the firewood. Grace tipped the bottle up and nearly drank half at one time.

She wiped her mouth, "Does anyone else know? Did your dad get caught? Where's your brother?" She fired question after question.

I tried to stay focused on what she was asking, but I couldn't take my eyes off her breasts. I adjusted myself in my jeans once again. Not wanting to scare her, any more than I probably already had, I continued, "Chris got so mad at him for killing Amy, he jumped him. Dad was so drunk by that time he couldn't even walk, much less defend himself. Chris was sitting on top of Dad and just kept punching and punching. I pulled him off at one point, but Chris picked up a large rock and hit me with it, knocking me out."

I then pulled back my hair and showed her the scar. That worked like a charm as she ran her small fingers across it. I leaned in and stole a kiss.

She pulled back, asking, "Then what?"

With a little sigh, I finished the story. "When I awoke, Dad's head was smashed in, and Chris was sitting against the front side of the cabin. While I was out, he killed Dad, sat down, and shot himself with his hunting rifle. They closed the case on Amy after finding what was left of her when they came to collect

Dad and Chris's bodies. Yet, the case of her brother is still an open investigation. I figured they really know, but no body, no proof. I miss my dad." I laid my head on her shoulder. As she took another drink, I tipped the bottom of the bottle higher in the air so that she would finish it off.

Grace decided she had to pee again. This time she most certainly needed my assistance. This time, she didn't even get away from the car. She pulled her shorts and panties down again, leaning against the rear car door. When she struggled to stand, I grabbed her. She stumbled about until she stepped entirely out of her shorts and panties. I sat her back in the front seat, handed her shorts to her, and slipped her panties in my pocket. I opened the glove box and pulled out a massive 8x12" sheet of condoms. I unzipped my pants and forced her hand on my cock. I asked her if she wanted some, showing her the condoms. She pulled away, telling me no, that she just wanted to go home.

Once back in the driver's seat, I leaned over onto her lap to get the seatbelt; not having anything on from the waist down, I couldn't help myself. I ran my tongue up her inner thigh, only stopping when she pushed me away. I buckled her in. After starting the engine, I slid my hand between her legs as far as possible and asked her if she was sure. She pushed me away again and muttered, "Stop!"

She reached for her shorts, which had fallen onto the floorboard. I picked them up and handed them to her, then pulled my hand away. "I had better get you home then." I just didn't say whose home.

The drive back to my trailer was a bit lengthy from where we had been, and my new playland, Miss Graceland, had passed out on the way. That made things much easier when we pulled up in front of the barn. I gently opened my door, got out, very easily pushed it just until the light went back off inside. I then went around to the trunk, snatching up a few zip ties and a rag.

Working my way over to the passenger side, I opened her door and zip-tied her wrists together and her ankles. As I unlocked her seatbelt, she started waking up. I then crammed the rag from the trunk into her mouth.

I picked her up and carried her into the barn. I was pretty proud of the system that I had rigged up before bringing Mazy home. I had installed two large pulleys in the rafters of the loft, then attached heavy chains. I placed Grace in the five-foot, flat basket that I had hooked to the ends of the chains and whisked her up into the loft. After I climbed up the ladder and pulled her out of the basket, I detached the chains.

She was beginning to struggle a bit, bringing me to the realization that I needed to get her confined quickly. Slipping a large dog collar around her neck, I connected it to one end of one of the chains. The other end, I tied off to the wall, limiting her mobility and making it easier to control her by a quick yank of the chain. I left the zip ties around her wrists and tightened them just a hair. To restrict her movement further, when I did choose to let her move, I had placed shackles on her ankles and attached them to the other chain. Once I felt confident that she was secure, I went into the trailer to relieve myself, have a beer, and watch a little TV to relax.

I woke up the next morning with the sunlight piercing through the window directly into my eyes. If I had lay there any longer, I'm sure I would have been nursing a sunburn. I made a pot of coffee, grabbed the last donut, then realized what I had done the night before. In all of the commotion with that damn girl, I forgot to bring in my beer and microwave dinners! Guess I could feed them to her, seeing as it's her fault they are thawed out and probably taste like crap now. I went out and got the food and beer out of the car, tossing them in the fridge.

I sat down with a cup of coffee, flipped the channel over to 3, and stopped on the news. The sports reports were being broadcasted, such as it was. Just telling us which games had been canceled again because the players and/or coaches had been infected. While watching the weather, I decided that a fire needed to be built, so I brought in some firewood. It was a little chilly in the trailer this morning. I paused in front of the set and grinned while they reported little Miss Graceland was missing.

While I continued about my business of building a fire, a special report came on.

Scientists have confirmed that with a simple blood-DNA test from those who had tested positive, individuals who had previously been infected by that particular mutated strand of the virus can be effectively traced.

The reporter added, "This is great progress. Identifying just how the virus is mutating means we are finally able to create an effective vaccine. Also, we can locate, notify, and treat infected people faster. This will allow quicker quarantines, fewer cases and transmission rate, and vaccinations before symptoms even occur." The reporter anxiously and excitedly continued, "We may finally be seeing an end to this pandemic very soon. Hang in there, guys, stay safe, social distance, wash your hands, wear your gloves, and by all means, wear your masks!"

I dismissed the report. When the fire took off, I slipped on my boots and headed out to the barn to play in my own little Graceland. When I climbed up the ladder, she was lying there in the straw, the gag still in her mouth, and tiny droplets of blood around her ankles that she had smeared over her feet, no doubt in an attempt to escape. Her wrists were raw, and she was missing a couple of her fake, bright red fingernails. I grabbed the chain attached to the wall and yanked it hard. She coughed. I was carrying the chain with me as I approached her, dragging it along, pulling on her throat, forcing her up onto her knees.

Feeling a bit generous, I allowed a little slack; she fell forward onto her twisted-together hands, still strapped together with the zip ties. I pulled the gag out of her mouth, yanked her head back by her lovely red hair, and gave her a drink of water.

I really liked this position. Not only was she chained up like a playful pup, but I proudly stood back and admired how she took so well to being on all fours. I secured the chain attached to the collar around her neck on a metal hoop I had installed and took a slow walk around her. I was frustrated when I got behind her because of those stupid shorts that she had managed to get back on in the car. They were blocking my full view.

With my dad's old 8" blade, hunting knife, I began to cut them off her. I was becoming more and more excited. Especially when she squealed out as the tip of the blade nicked her pretty little ass.

She yelled out, "I have to pee! I have to pee! Please, I'll do whatever you want but just let me pee first!"

HMMMM, I thought to myself, I was never into golden showers, so I unshackled her ankles and tossed a brand-new metal bucket at her, hitting her in the face. "Hurry up!" I told her, as I was about to bust, with anticipation. "I'm ready to play in Graceland." I laughed out loud.

I sat down and watched eagerly as she struggled to pull what remained of her shorts off—then perched that pretty thing over the bucket. I took off my shirt, began to unzip my pants when she fell to the side, pulling the collar hard against her throat. Wow, how freaking hot was that? My girl will even strangle herself for kicks. I have to admit, I did get pissed off when she knocked over the bucket of pee. I shoved her over and began trying to soak it up with the gag from her mouth. Fighting against the chains and collar that choked her, she managed to get back up onto her knees. Pushing her head down, forcing her back to all fours, now bare-bottomed, I grabbed her from behind and knelt down behind her. That damn woman grabbed the metal bucket and knocked my ass to the loft floor.

I vaguely remember seeing flashes of her grabbing the chain above her head and pulling herself up. She swung around on the chain, wrapped her soft legs around my head, and for a moment, I thought, hell yeah, heaven! Then I blacked out. The next thing I remember is waking up on the barn floor below the loft. Jason was standing over me, arguing with his nosey girlfriend.

"What happened?" I asked.

Jason proceeded to tell me, "We saw enormous amounts of black smoke rolling up the hill as never before, so we came down to check on you. When we got here, we saw what was left of your trailer. Pretty much a total loss, dude. Just the frame covered in the charred remnants of what used to be."

"Grace, did you see Grace?" I asked, still in a state of fumbling confusion.

"Is that the girl we heard screaming through the woods?" Jason's girlfriend asked. "What did you do to her?'

Rubbing blood from the side of my head, I explained, "Yeah, she was into some kinky stuff," I replied.

Jason held out his hand to help me to my feet and said, "Dude, she's gone, and she didn't look like she had enjoyed her evening with you. If I were you, I'd go find that girl."

"Let her go, that crazy bitch," I gruffed in anger as I kicked the bucket that had fallen to the barn floor with me.

I spent the next two months living with Jason and his woman while the insurance investigators decided if they were going to pay out or not. I wasn't sure if Grace caught the place on fire when she escaped or if I was careless and forgot to close the door on the wood burner. I went back and cleaned out the barn, again getting rid of all evidence of my date with Grace. I told Jason what sucked; after losing my trailer, I didn't even get laid. I had no idea just how much the situation really sucked.

New Year's Day, 2023, I was busy nursing a hangover when they came. There is nothing like blue lights and loud sirens at 5:00 AM to make a man feel like his head was in a vise. They burst through Jason's door, put me in cuffs, and stuffed me in the back of the squad car. When we pulled up to the station, I wondered if they were taking me in regarding the investigation on my trailer. Nope, it was clear when they drugged me into the barred-glass side of the building; I was going to jail.

Come to find out, little Miss Grace Lynn had become infected with the virus. Just my luck, her case was one of the first to be used in contact tracing through blood testing. Her strand of the virus held my DNA. She had told them everything that had happened that night and confessed to burning down my trailer when she couldn't find a working phone. She told them she hoped the flames would signal the fire department and rescue, but I live too far out for that. The only reason it took them so long to find me was that the dumbass got lost in the woods and couldn't tell them how to get to my property.

Of course, I argued that just because the virus had my DNA attached didn't mean she got it directly from me, nor did it prove what she had said was true. I explained that we had both been drinking, and she was into some serious kinky stuff. I was just trying to oblige her. The authorities refuted, saying that she still had the gag rag with her. The rag was tested and found not just my DNA, not just Grace's DNA, but Mazy's DNA too. Plus, they had found the DNA of Amy and her brother exactly where Grace told them it would be.

As if all that wasn't bad enough, the kicker is, I now sit here on death row. They are pinning it all on me; they are now blaming me not just for Amy's brother's death but also Mazy's death, and now it seems they got me for one more. You see, little Miss Graceland just passed away from complications of the virus. "Well, damn! She too was a feisty, little, hot thing."

Chapter Six – Secrets

It Tastes Lovely

Survival is survival

Don't deny me because I'm different

All humanity sucks life from something

You are not superior for buying your food

Substance is substance

Dining on prepared flesh

Skinned, flayed, chopped, it is still flesh

Yet prepared with seasonings and tossed upon flames

Flesh is flesh

Did you devour the clean or unclean

Do you know the difference, does the difference matter

Sauteed, saturated with blood

Meat is meat

Once carried oxygen through the very veins that gave life

You placed on your tongue and shredded by tooth

Consumed with great satisfaction

Pleasure is pleasure

Whether raw, rare or burnt

Your body benefited

Your mouth delighted as you did partake

Momma's Beast

I felt guilty when Momma died. I didn't cry at her funeral; I didn't feel any sorrow. I don't know how I felt. I guess I was kind of scared, like when I was a kid lying in bed at night listening to Momma crying from the next room. My father died when I was six, and I had become her favorite; maybe because I was the baby. Who knows what thoughts ran through that woman's head at night? The others had a hard life, sharing everything from bedrooms and clothes to even food and friends. They were all much older than I was. I had two sisters and one brother; well, the second one died, so they said. He was supposedly my twin, who didn't survive the experience of birth. I have heard the stories and even Stephen King's nod to one twin absorbing another. I sometimes wonder what had happened to him.

After she passed away, I was the only one to come back. I suppose because I was the youngest and last to leave the house. The others never returned once they got out, not even for family gatherings or holidays. I couldn't help but harbor hard feelings toward them. I know life wasn't easy, but how could they turn their backs entirely on her, who struggled so desperately to provide? It couldn't have been easy for her either.

Yes, I know people gossiped about her because she worked as a stripper, or an entertainer, as she called it. Yes, I know the man she brought in once in a while after my father passed away was a bit on the abusive side. However, that didn't make her masochistic, as my oldest sister claimed. She did what she had to do to make sure we all had what we needed. She even managed to give us many of the things we just wanted. Regardless of my siblings' and even outsiders' opinions, she was a good Momma. She loved us deeply. She gave up all of her dreams and even opportunities for us.

Three days elapsed since she died, and I was at the house

alone. Someone had to sort through all those memories left behind. The thoughts of everything from my Momma's life to my childhood, being rummaged through by strangers, was disturbing. While sorting through this and that, these and those, I found a box under her bed. Sifting through papers, clippings of our first locks of hair, photos, and more, I found a document that would change my entire perspective and ultimately my life. The old yellowed sheet of paper read:

My son, Esau, is in the basement. I named him that, as the son who feared to be left behind, from the Bible. He has been there since birth. I couldn't let anyone see him because of his gross deformities and mental retardation. I still love him, though. I don't know why but I love that lil' beast. I was scared to let him live like the other boys because people are so cruel. I couldn't let them use my beast as a target for their manipulations, harsh treatments, and inhumane tortures that have become the societal norms. He would not be someone to pick on, just something to become another mere demonstration of disparagement in an already screwed-up world.

I bought him toys to play with and tried my best to set up his special bedroom in the basement. I keep him locked downstairs because I knew that the others would be afraid of his appearance and not understand him. Besides, how horrible would it be to be disowned even by his own siblings. I knew that would create even more significant harm, being turned away by his own family.

When I die, please let loose my precious baby Esau, my beast. Give my boy safe passage and protection.

After I read the paper, I saw a small key taped to the back. We in the house were not permitted to go near the basement door. Momma was now gone, and I just had to see what my brother looked like, assuming he was even still in there. After ripping the key from the page, I went downstairs and stopped in the kitchen entrance. I just glared across the room to that basement door. I couldn't move. Questions raced through my mind like mice through a maze, dazed and confused. Could this be for real? How could I have spent seventeen years in this same house, never knowing another human being, my twin brother, was living in the basement?

My mother had always been a creative soul and an aspiring author; maybe this was just an elaborate ruse. Maybe, just maybe, this imaginary child was her muse. Could she have made this all up in a sad attempt for fortune and fame as a would-be writer? I moved over to the tiny kitchen island that was accompanied by two small bar stools. I slid one out and sat down while trying to conjure up memories of our past.

Now that I think about it, several years after Pops died, strange murders started happening around our area. I don't recall them as they occurred, yet I remember the lingering reports that would occasionally surface. You know how the news doesn't have anything worthy to report on current events, so they occasionally grasp backward into their vaults? Well, those are the stories I remember. I guess that would have put me and this supposed twin around age ten when they were first reported.

I do remember one broadcast like it was yesterday. A special report interrupted my Saturday morning cartoons and a hot bowl of Cream of Wheat. The woman's dark hair and red lips burned into my mind as she said, "A decade after the outbreak, a mutilated body was found in City Park. Police suspect it could have been from a relapsed, infected predator." I had no idea what she meant then, but odd how it invaded my thoughts at the very moment I learned about a potential beast in Momma's basement. Could there be some connection? This is ludicrous, I thought to myself. Even if my twin brother was in that basement, he's still my brother, my family, and none of us are crazy enough for that kind of shit!

At this point, I was too nervous about opening that basement door. Curiosity got the best of me, so I went back upstairs to Momma's room. I riffled through her hope chest, which sat at the foot of her bed, not wanting to believe there was a person, my brother no less, locked in the basement of this now empty house. A place I used to call home. I had to find proof, a birth certificate, pictures, a locket of hair, anything to prove this wasn't just one of Momma's creepy stories. I pulled out her old wedding dress, which was stained with age. An ugly red and green crocheted afghan that Grandma had made, and an old, wooden, engraved box. I sat the box gently on the floor as if it would break and opened it slowly with great anticipation. A gun! It was a damn gun! An excellent damn gun, just like you would expect to see straight out of *Dodge City*, but a gun! Only a twenty-two at that! Not what I was searching for! So, I closed the box, slid it across the floor in frustration, and kept digging.

Then I ran across an old manilla envelope. I chuckled to myself as I pulled it out, recalling how as a kid, I called them vanilla envelopes, thinking maybe somewhere in the world, there were chocolate versions. It was super thick and cumbersome. This must have been what I had been searching for. I sat upon Momma's bed. I blew and then wiped the dust off onto the knotty white quilt that was trimmed in tassels and then broke open the seal. Yep, just as I suspected, all sorts of old documents and a couple of disconcerting baby photos. His head was caved in on the left side as if someone had crushed it with a ball bat. His left eye socket, which held a barely visible eyeball, was adjacent to his nostrils. The bottom jaw projected out like a piranha, and what infant already has teeth? I dropped the photos and jumped back. How could this thing be my twin?

I took a deep breath and gathered my thoughts. In an attempt to regain my composure, I proceeded in my search for actual answers. There had to be more details on not just my brother but my siblings. In addition to the stupid virus that had swept the world, even the murders, something, anything, other than these gross pictures. Yet what I found, among the papers, was my brother's birth certificate:

Esau Chevon Crouts, born on this day of December twelve, Nineteen hundred and seventy-three. 3 pounds and 8 ounces. 12 and ¾ inches long. Mother Alicia Kris Crouts, Father Chevon Adam Crouts.

Under the birth certificate was a photo of Momma and Pops on their wedding day. She looked so happy with her little hippie, floral halo, and simple straight, short, lace gown. Sorting through the small stack of faded photos, I saw my grandparents and even a few of my siblings between the thin paper prints to thick polaroid shots. But while trying to discern whose baby photo was whose because all relations share certain features, I could not identify myself in any. How was I her favorite, yet there be no actual evidence in this box of my existence?

Then I found Momma's diary. As I opened the black leather binder, a hangnail caught on the worn cover. I began to gnaw at it, scraping my teeth along the edge, trying to save the nail but just eliminate the protruding annoyance. As I flipped the cover open and turned to the second page where the writings began, I ripped the entire white edge off my nail, and it got stuck between my teeth. As I read Momma's most profound thoughts, I started picking at the first piece of my nail from my teeth with my middle finger. Although I was successful in dislodging the first, it resulted in my losing a second.

My fingertips felt raw from the missing nails, almost as if a busted blister had revealed new sensitive skin. Anyone who is a true nail-biter knows exactly the feeling I'm talking about. It kind of hurts, but it really doesn't; instead, it only felt unusually awkward. Very similar to the information I just read in her diary. My oldest siblings were not my siblings. They were not even blood. The leftover, rough, jagged edge was still an annoyance, just like learning my siblings were all foster kids, not even adopted. As I continued reading about the truths of my family, I gnawed on the nail even further and further back. I exposed more and more of the precious innocent skin underneath while exposing more and more hidden secrets of my family.

As I read and flipped page after page, allowing each skeleton to fall out of Momma's diary, finally, there I was! On page fifteen!

My sweet Emelia Christine, Esau's fraternal twin. I thank the good Lord that she was a healthy five pounds, five ounces, and beautifully perfect. She has all ten fingers and all ten toes, unlike Esau, who was missing a few of each. Her lovely symmetrical blue eyes are positioned exactly where they should be, on each side of the bridge of her perfect little nose. She has the purest, smoothest complexion as if God Himself had wrapped the flesh over her meticulously designed skeleton and skull. She was nothing like the beast that was sucking precious life from her in my womb. She was healthy, but she was pale and weak. I suppose throughout the pregnancy, she had to have been so strong for so long that the birth damn near took away her little life. They barely let me touch them after birth. They swooped both of my babies from my body and took them directly to the NICU.

Once again, I became uncomfortable with Momma's words. I mean, I was grateful that I was healthy and that she loved me. However, calling my brother a beast just because he was different was appalling. How could she speak of her own baby, my brother, that way? I tossed the diary on the end of the bed. I needed a drink. I went back down into the kitchen and poked around in the cabinets. One thing about Momma, she always kept a bottle or two hidden here and there. Under the kitchen sink, I found a large bottle of whiskey. Not my first choice but it would do. I grabbed a glass of ice, poured the whiskey over, and added some pop. I sat back down at the island and just stared at the basement door.

So many memories were running through my head, very few with my older siblings; ha! Not my siblings, just other kids that lived in this house for a short while. No wonder they all left as soon as they could. No wonder they are not here now. They probably felt like they didn't belong, any more than the beast in the basement. I wondered if they knew about him. I wondered if that's why they all left so quickly. I wondered if that's why they won't come back now.

I got up, finished off the drink, and walked over to the basement door. I was curious if he was still down there. I leaned my ear against the door in an attempt to hear him, hear anything. Nothing, not even vibrations from the furnace or water pipes. I fixed another drink and turned to go back upstairs. I paused in the doorway, looked back at the bottle of whiskey on the island, and grabbed it; as I tucked it under my arm, I went back up to Momma's room.

Sitting back down on the bed, I placed my drink and the bottle on the nightstand beside me. I remembered that old nightstand, dark and ugly, something no doubt from the 1970s. I recalled it being full of prescription bottles and a dirty, amber-colored glass ashtray. She said the pills were prescribed by the doctor for depression and anxiety, but thinking back now, who the hell is that depressed? I grabbed her diary and dove back into Momma's memories.

It came time for my release from the cold sterilized hospital.

They told me that they wanted to keep Esau, but I could take Emelia home. I was not leaving without both of my babies. I convinced the doctor to let him come home with me if I promised to take him to the pediatrician the next day. Once we got them home, Emelia did very well, eating like a horse and pooping regularly. However, Esau was struggling. The pediatrician wanted to put him back in the NICU. I told her that I would take him back the following day. When the sun rose the next day, he began nursing and seemed to be getting stronger by the hour. I decided he needed me more than he needed the doctors. However, they told me I could get in trouble, even arrested, if I didn't take him back. So, I did what I felt was best for my beast and told them that he had passed away through the night.

My husband, Adam, was good buddies with Mike Caid; he owned the local crematory and funeral home. We explained to him what was going on, and after he came for a visit and saw Esau, he agreed to sign off on the death certificate. He said it was probably just a matter of time anyway, and at least he could stay at home with his family. So as far as the rest of the world was concerned, Esau was dead. Which I still believe was the best thing for him because as he grew, it became clear he had grave mental and developmental issues. No matter how hard I tried to teach him, he couldn't even understand how to eat with his hands or walk on his feet. He would just crawl around on all fours like a dog.

I was shocked; I couldn't believe my parents wouldn't get him the help he needed. Maybe, if they had taken him back to the hospital, they could have done corrective surgeries. In addition, perhaps if they had gotten him help, someone could have assisted him with teaching and essential life skills. I loved Momma, but she wasn't exactly of the elegant, proper sort. She also wasn't very patient, so I'm sure she wouldn't have been the best teacher or even mother for a child with special needs. I blamed her for my brother's disposition.

My anger began to boil once again; I grabbed my drink and sucked down nearly half. I just didn't understand how she could be so dumb! Truth be told, I wonder now, if all those damn pills on her nightstand years ago weren't the cause of my brother's deformities. I wished she were here now. So many questions I wanted to ask. Honestly, I just wanted to shout at her for the next ten years or so. So help me, my sweet Lord, if this was true ... I just didn't know what I would do.

I threw the diary back onto the bed. After finishing off my drink, I poured a little more whiskey in the glass over the shrinking ice. I took a deep sigh and walked around the bedroom. Sipping on the now straight-up in my cup, I paused at every photo on her wall. My so-called older siblings in a group portrait. One of Momma and Pops back in their dating days, a picture of me in my ankle-length, green Easter dress: each was giving the impression of a happy home. What a crock! I thought. My whole life has been based on lies and wretched, even criminal deeds. Who the hell was this woman, my Momma? I have no doubts now that the others must have known what she and Pops had done. I used to question the other kids' love and loyalty to Momma, but maybe their just walking away was their idea of loyalty. However, I just couldn't fathom how any of this could be construed as any form of love.

I sucked down drink number three, absent of soda, and grabbed the key again. Unsure if this was all real, hoping deep within my core that it was just a story that she had dreamed up in her sick, twisted mind, I ambled down the old wooden staircase hesitantly, stopping every two or three creaky steps, grasping the key in a tight fist against my breast. I ran my hand along the smooth, dark-wood railing, looking beyond to the foot of the staircase. I reimagined our tiny Christmas tree, adorned with those ugly silver strands of shiny ribbons the old-timers called tinsel. Lit up by the large two-inch tall bulbs. It's a wonder the house didn't catch on fire. I came to the end of the steps and that spun around to where the tree would have stood. Beside the old staircase, just opposite of the huge bay window, images of gifts from the past piled one on top of another and not one with the name of Esau or even beast.

The animosity welling up within was creating a new-found hatred for Momma. Passing the memories of Christmases past, walking to the right, through the hall, and into the kitchen, I found myself numb. I caught myself against the island, realizing part of this temporary paralysis could be from the whiskey, as well as the anger, confusion, and fear. People frequently throw the phrase *paralyzed with fear* into novels, stories, conversations, and even into the air, but have they truly experienced that? I did. My breath snatched from my chest; my legs went limp, my heart nearly busted out, right through bone and flesh; it was the greatest fear I had ever experienced.

Once I collected myself, I moved on to the basement door. Not knowing what I would face, I grabbed the largest knife from the block on the counter and twisted the key in the lock. With a downward jerk, it broke open. I tossed the lock on the counter and opened the door. Chills ran up my arms and spine as I flipped the light switch on and began to descend into my brother's room. It smelled awful. I felt a cool, damp breeze hit me, almost like a towel snapped across the face with a dirty wet rag. It took my breath, stung just a bit, and made me shiver in my step. The boards pretending to be stairs were very steep, old, split, and narrow. Some even had large holes in spots as if big rats had burrowed through them.

As I came to the bottom, I could feel the hard concrete beneath my feet, even through my thin-soled shoes. It was still very dark, as the light only illuminated the old unsteady staircase. "Esau?" I whispered into the darkness. "Esau, I am Emelia. I am your sister. Esau, I am here to help you." From the furthest, darkest corner, I heard what seemed to be chains dragging across the concrete and a gurgling noise like a clogged toilet. I felt around the walls, running my hands through cobwebs, along rough timbers of wood beams, searching for another light switch. With no luck, I pulled out my cell phone and turned on the flashlight.

Walking slowly toward the sound of the chains sliding back and forth, trying to focus my eyes into that dark corner, I hit my head. It was an old dangling light fixture, specifically, an old socket hanging from loose wires with a light bulb attached. I turned my phone toward the bulb and carefully searched for a chain or switch. Neither being found, I decided to twist the bulb; as I did, the light flickered and came on with a steady soft glow. The small electrical hazard immediately cast light into the corner and onto Momma's beast.

I gasped at the sight of him. I may have even released a bit of an unexpected scream because he jumped back upon his little bed, as a terrified child would do. It was incredibly too small; as my twin, he too would be forty-seven now, and yet his safe haven was a small race-car bed. He seemed more of a frightened toddler than a grown man or even a monstrous beast, as Momma called him. Yet, maybe in empathy and somewhat still buried innocence, I lost sight of the fact that, human or not, my brother or not, he was still Momma's beast. A beast that had been locked away in a basement for forty-seven years.

I slowly approached him, instinctively holding my hand out, like one would do to a strange dog just before attempting to pet it. My first contact with my brother was a gasp, a scream, and then holding my hand out to him like a dog. What was wrong with me? I wanted to love him, yet I was still treating him like a monstrosity of a wild animal. So, I pulled my hand back, then extended both arms out as if I was going to embrace him in a hug. He slowly approached me, crawling off his bed onto the cold floor. He stayed on his hands and knees while he sniffed around the edge of my feet. Feeling like a total dumbass, I put my arms down and, with one hand, reached out to him. He bit my middle finger and ran back onto his bed. He began to growl like an old black bear.

I decided to rethink this a bit more. At best, I needed to read more of Momma's diary to find out how to care for him. Clearly, I couldn't call the authorities. They would take him away and just lock him up in some unforgiving institution, with people who didn't see him as a brother, a son, or family. I envisioned people caring for him as if he was a morphed creature chained and caged in a zoo or circus freak show. Yet, in some sense, that's really what he had become. So, I spoke softly to him, "Esau, I am your sister. Our Momma, your Momma, has passed on. She is no longer here. She will never be able to come back. I'm all you have. You have to let me take care of you. Just let me love you."

I looked around for a table, dishes, food, or water, but all I saw were two very large metal bowls on the floor. They actually looked like flat hubcaps. I asked him if these were his plates and if he was hungry. He jumped off the bed, smacked his hands on the edges of them, flipping them both into the air, lunging them in my direction. "Okay, I'll be back," I said as I picked up his hubcap style plates and left that creepy basement. Back in the kitchen, I just closed the door, not locking it behind me. Momma had him in chains anyway. I started searching through the cabinets and refrigerator, this time seeking for something to feed Esau. Not having much luck with my search for food, I did manage to find some witch hazel to disinfect my finger and wrapped a large Band-Aid around it.

With the cabinets nearly bare, I sat back down at the island and sighed. I didn't think I could do this. I didn't know if I could even deal with the emotional train wreck that was about to hit me. Much less take care of him. I pulled out my phone and sent a text to my girlfriend, Judy.

I have discovered something horrible

It's my family

I'm not sure what to do.

I laid my phone on the island and went back upstairs to get the bottle and Momma's diary. When I returned, Judy had replied several times. My phone had lit up like that old Christmas tree with notifications of texts and missed calls. I opened the texts.

Hey babe, what's going on?

R u ok?

U literally just texted me!

What's going on?

Please answer me!

Before I could reply, she called again. There was no real conversation, a simple "Hello," from me and …

"I'm already on my way" from her.

Curious, if she gets here and sees what crazy looks like, will she still love me? Will she stay and help or run in the other direction? Is our relationship worth the hassle of society condemning us as a couple, in addition to Momma's beast? Will she walk away in complete fear with anticipation that I may turn into my beastly twin? She can't come here! She can't be a witness to this! These are now my deep dark secrets, not just Momma's anymore.

I poured another shot of straight-up whiskey in my cup, this time adding a few of the last cubes of ice from the tray to my glass. I sat back down on the stool, which seemed to want to run away from me at this point. What was I going to feed him? There was nothing in the house. I wondered if he'd like pizza; I thought, I could go for some pizza. I revisited the diary looking for clues to his favorite foods, when I stumbled upon a disturbing entry about Momma nursing him.

I'm not sure I made the right choice by letting everyone that could have helped us think he died. Adam just brought me to the ER, and I am about to undergo emergency surgery. While nursing Esau in the middle of the night, just after Emelia fed, Esau became very aggressive. He bit down on my breast. He shouldn't, but for some reason, he already has very sharp pointed teeth. He took my whole nipple and a chunk of my right breast. The doctors worried about blood loss and infection, but all I could think of was how will I continue to nurse my two babies.

Wow, I couldn't even imagine trying to nurse him. I saw those teeth in his newborn photos, and I was just dumbfounded that she would have even tried. I discovered that she ended up having her right breast removed. Furthermore, the federally funded medical insurance that she was on did not pay for cosmetic plastic surgery, so she never had reconstruction done. I was beginning to understand all of those bottles of meds on her nightstand now. I was surprised that she didn't completely lose it with all of this and then Pops dying. I took another sip of my drink and decided I needed to slow down. So, I poured a bit of pop on top and sipped again. While flipping through the pages of the diary, the doorbell rang. I rushed to open the old mahogany door, and there stood my lovely Judy. When she stepped inside, I fell into her firm embrace, breaking down in tears.

I led her into the kitchen and pulled out the other little stool for her to sit on at the island. While fixing her a drink, I told her the whole story. I cringed at every morbid detail, with horror in my soul and embarrassment across my face. I should have anticipated her response. A bit of a late-blooming *Hippie* she was, practicing lagom--Momma would have loved her. Judy believes in Yin and Yang and thrives on maintaining a balance between positive and negative energy in life.

She simply sighed, pulled the diary across the island in front of her, and asked, "Is this it?"

I nodded yes, as I handed her the drink. I sat down on the stool beside her, permitting her to dive into my family's horror story.

When she had skimmed through enough, she looked at me and said, "Damn, Emm. I'm so sorry." She leaned over and hugged me while rubbing her warm hands up and down my back.

I explained that I had been down there and was trying to figure out what to feed him. "I'm pretty hungry too," I added with a half-smile.

Pulling out her cell phone, she asked, "Chinese or Pizza?"

I kind of laughed and replied, "Well, let's leave *covid* out of this and do Italian!"

She laughed and called in two large pizzas with pepperoni, extra cheese, bacon, and banana peppers.

I looked at her inquisitively, "Two Large?"

She smiled with her reply, "The beast hasn't eaten for at least three days. I'm sure that man is hungry."

I stood up from my stool, moved in between her legs, and held her close. "Thank you," I whispered in her ear.

She pushed me back just slightly to look at me, taking both sides of my face in her hands, and announced, "Babe, I'm in it. I love you. Whatever you face, I face. We will figure this out. It will take more than skeletons, secrets, and even the boogeyman to keep me away from you."

I slowly sat back on my stool, and she slid her hand across

my thigh, giving two pats, as she took a drink. She kept glaring at the basement door as we talked about all I had discovered. I sat quietly for a moment as she fanned through the diary, stopping on one page that caught her eye.

I have genuinely been apprehensive over the years about Esau and his appetite. But tonight, scared me. I mean yeah, I've heard on the news about these murders in the area; but honestly, I just figured it was someone that had been infected with this virus or, worse, experienced the newly reported side effects from the vaccine. Neither here nor there, I haven't been exposed to either, so neither could he have been. But!!!!

I have been letting him loose through the cellar doors now and then so that he could roam around and get some fresh air. For the last few months, there have been no problems. However, tonight when he came back, he was covered in what appeared to be blood. Maybe he just grabbed a squirrel or something while he was out. He hasn't been eating the food I've been cooking for the rest of the family, so maybe he's just hungry. I mean, I don't know what to do. I've been very dedicated to being a good mom and cooking every night, everything from chili, enchiladas, chicken, and rice to even pizza night. He won't eat any of it. What is he eating then?

"You may need to read this, babe," Judy said softly.

"What is it?" I asked.

She handed me the diary, and I reread Momma's words. "Yes! I remember that!" I shouted excitedly yet immediately became frigid. Yes, I thought, I do remember that. I remember that red-lipped newscaster interrupting my hot cereal and cartoons. Yes! Oh no, could it be? Could there be a connection? Thank the good Lord, the doorbell rang again. This time I sat and sipped and let Judy get it. A few minutes later, she came back carrying two large pizza boxes and sat them on the counter parallel to the island.

"Your Momma have any plates in this kitchen?" she asked.

"Um, yeah, but just grab those paper plates off the microwave," I replied.

Judy slid a couple of pieces of pizza on each plate and handed me one. She sat back down beside me, and as we ate, we continued to put the pieces of Momma's diary together. "It must have been him," I said.

Judy smiled with a quick jerk of her head to the right and replied, "Maybe, maybe not. Let's just eat, and then we will take the other pizza down to him."

After we finished eating, we both held up our glasses of whiskey and pop, said a little cheer, and chugged it down like fraternity boys. Judy grabbed the other pizza box in one hand and my shirttail in the other. We headed down the steps. I cautioned her on each step, explaining about the rotting boards beneath our feet. When we approached Esau, he jumped down off his bed and lunged toward us. Only his chains stopped him a few feet from us and Judy dropped the pizza box. I picked it up, opened the box, and slid it over in front of him.

Judy was clinging to the back of my shirt with a death grip. Esau jumped into the box and dove his sharp, vampire-like teeth into the pizza. After a few snarls and tears into the toppings, he backed off. "Esau, I don't know what you like to eat, but you need to eat something. Please."

He then slid the box of pizza across the floor, so hard it flipped up onto my legs. Judy whispered in my ear, "Maybe we should just go."

I overturned the box, shoving the pizza back inside it. Then I slid the box back against his little bed and said, "Fine! You stubborn ass! But you better keep this because I'm not letting you out!" I was mad. I turned, grabbing Judy by the hand, and we headed back to the steps.

When we got back upstairs, I realized I was terrified not of my brother but of losing Judy. I looked fear in the face and asked my beloved, "Are you sure? Are you sure you want to deal with everything that may await me?" I flipped off the light, slammed the door shut, and locked it back behind us.

"Yes, I will stay by your side and we will do this together. Who knows, it may just make for a great movie someday," she replied with a burst of soft laughter.

The next day, Judy and I both really jumped into Momma's room. Not one photo or paper went without examination by at least one of us. We discovered that there was an outbreak in the mid-1970s. Some kind of unknown virus was suspected of having been brought to the U.S. via war vets. This could have been what truly affected Esau and possibly the cause of Pops' death. The newspapers we found said that some people that were infected had an uncontrollable hunger for raw meat. However, they claimed it was contained to the initial outbreak cities and eventually conquered through vaccines.

That was odd, as more recent papers have reported that this new outbreak was creating deformities in newborns that were refusing to take even their mother's milk. Could this new strain have come back to life from the 70s? I wondered if the current pandemic was a result of surviving victims of the first. Curious if Momma letting Esau loose was the cause of this new outbreak that seems to have morphed, as the virus at hand so far has been restricted to just our county.

"Judy," I began to say when she interrupted.

"Yes! I think so too. But Emm, if he is the cause of the new pandemic, he could also be the cure. We have to call the authorities and report all of this. Who knows, maybe he has infected us!"

I shook my head and replied, "No, babe, I don't think so. I believe it was the first responders, the M.E., the coroners, etc., that he has infected. I've got an idea!"

With fear and confusion across her face, she asked, "What?"

I then explained my theory to her in more detail. If Esau created this new outbreak, then it should be pretty easy to trace. It would take some research, but I believed the two of us could find the answers. We just needed to check to see if Momma's diary correlated with when she let him out compared to the reported deaths in the area. Then further research on the first responders, the medical examiner, coroner, any doctors or nurses present and then a comparison of their records to the more recent births with the infection. Meanwhile, we needed to figure out what to feed the beast.

Several weeks passed, and we were able to prove my theory. Momma's entries in her diary when she let Esau out did indeed coincide with the murders that occurred. The births of the infected newborns were easily traced back to those who had some type of contact with Esau's victims.

I haven't let him loose. Instead, we have been feeding him raw hamburger, steak, and pork chops. Judy even threw a couple of live chickens down there as a joke, but he consumed them too. Okay, he may be my brother, he may be my blood, but Momma was right. He is also a monstrous, wild beast!

I have moved back into Momma's house, giving up my apartment, and Judy stays here with me several nights a week. I know we can't go on like this, but I don't know what to do with him. I can feel Judy pulling further and further away from me, and I can't blame her. Yet, he will let me approach him now, so that's a positive. He even occasionally tries to rub his head against my legs as a stray cat will do for attention and food. Judy still wants to call the authorities, but I am on the fence. I mean, deep in my heart, I know that's what we need to do. I realize they may be able to find a cure for this once and for all if they have him in custody to run tests on. They could even create a more efficient vaccine to prevent future breakouts, but he's still my brother, and I don't want him to be poked and prodded like a lab rat.

Yesterday gave birth to more than just a new day; it brought forth a new sort of pain. One, I'm not sure I will be able to side-step or move past. After work, I came in and fed Esau as usual. We made a little more progress, as I could sit on his little bed while he ate. He even let me sponge-bathe him for a few minutes before he snapped at me. His back is covered in hair, and it reminds me of the wolfman. Anyway, I disinfected and wrapped the new bite on my arm, then put dinner on. I poured a glass of Chardonnay and was sitting on Momma's ugly, flowered sofa watching her old TV with rabbit ears up when Judy walked in.

"Hey, babe! I got dinner on, and Esau has been fed and kind of bathed. How was your day?" I said with a smile. She sat down beside me and took my hands in hers. She moved away from me when I tried to lean in to kiss her. "What's going on?" I asked in a terrified voice.

She took a deep sigh, released her light grip on my hands, and said, "We have a problem. Emm, you need to call and report Esau so they can come to get him. We cannot keep doing this, and the news is reporting that this new virus is spreading throughout the state. We need a cure!"

I shrugged her off, tapped her hands, and reassured her they would find one, just like they did before. But she was resistant, determined that I report him. She continued, "It's come down to this -- you turn him in, or I'm moving back home to Cali with my mom."

Being one stubborn bitch, who was now hurt like hell, who always bucks against ultimatums, simply replied, "No! Do what you have to do, I'm going to bed!" I took the food off the burner, tossed it all into the sink, and went to bed alone.

I don't understand what Judy's new urgency is about, but making me choose between her and my brother was utterly unfair. Yeah, I know he's not like other people, but he's still a person! Besides, she promised she would stand beside me through all of this, but now she's backtracking. I sit and ponder if she would do what she is asking me to do if this was her brother. I'm so mad and so hurt, I feel betrayed! Well, she can pack her shit and just leave then! I don't care.

What I didn't realize was just how betrayed I felt. The next day she did come to collect the things she had brought here. We exchanged a few choice words that ended in her leaving and us both in tears. I thought that was the end of it, but I thought wrong. I got dressed, fed the beast a roll of raw sausage, and went on to work. When I came home, I noticed Judy's car in the driveway. At first I thought she had come back, but then I saw a police car, an ambulance, and a large, black SUV parked on the side street along the corner of my drive. What had she done?

I busted through my Momma's front door like the FBI on a raid! "JUDY! Where are you? What's going on?"

I rushed to the basement door, and sure enough, it was open. I jetted down those old decrepit steps to find Judy lying at the bottom. The cellar doors going outside had been completely demolished with a policeman hanging over the edge of the concrete steps. He was dangling from his tie that appeared to have been caught in the hinges of the cellar doors. To the right, the beast was gone. One of his broken chains was wrapped around another officer's neck as he, too, lay lifeless but on the floor in front of his race car bed. I rushed to Judy, pulling her up into my arms. I can't even describe how I felt between the sheer heartbreak to the anger of real betrayal.

I held her tightly against my breast. "Dammit! Judy, Dammit! It didn't have to come to this! You guys provoked him! Dammit, Judy!" I yelled as I squeezed her as tight as I could.

As I squeezed harder she began to gasp for air. "Oh, lawd! Judy! Breathe baby, breathe!" I pulled out my phone and called 911. "Hold on, baby. Help is coming. Hold on."

I saw the blood gushing from her shoulder and arm. I laid her back down gently and tried to tear off the edge of my skirt. That shit you see in movies, yeah, it's just in movies; material does not tear that easy. I stood up and took my skirt off, and wrapped up her shoulder, filling in the gaping hole between what was left of her arm. It was like Esau took her actual shoulder and a large portion of her upper arm in one bite. Looking at the officers still here, I knew beyond a doubt, if Esau wanted to kill her, he could have. Despite his swift rampage, pressured by time for a speedy escape, the way those chains were broken, he could have taken us both out at any time he chose, but he didn't.

Of course, they wouldn't let me go with Judy to the hospital because of the spread. Besides, I wasn't family or her wife. Well, I can't be her wife because those assholes in political offices won't allow it. They were insistent that I go to the police station to answer their questions. I told them everything and even turned over the photos and Momma's diary. They finally agreed with me that none of this was my fault and allowed me to leave.

It was several days after Judy's surgery before they would let me in to see her. The staff even suited me up like an alien invader before I could go in. They made me stay six feet away from her bed, but at least we could talk. At first, I was concerned about her recovery. I mean, she had lost a lot of blood. The doctors weren't able to save her arm; they had to amputate it. I was mad, asking her why she betrayed me that way. If she hadn't done that, none of this would have happened. She would still have her arm, my brother wouldn't be loose to hurt others, and the police wouldn't be hunting him down with orders to kill. She had made a mess of all this.

Then the doctor came in to give her an update on all of the test results. "Ma'am, you may want to be alone while I give you these results," he suggested, giving me the cue to leave.

"No, this is my girlfriend, and it involves her and her brother anyway. So please go ahead." She spoke with confidence.

"Oh, well, that is a very liberal outlook and strategy for life. Okay, well, you have tested positive for the virus. We do have a trial vaccine, but because of your pregnancy, we cannot administer it to you. If you had still been in your first trimester, we might have been able to, but because you are at 18 weeks, it's against the law. However, we will keep you here and monitor your condition, especially since you have recently suffered from such trauma and amputation; you will be with us for a while anyway. We will do all we can to keep you and your baby safe."

I had been leaning against the wall; as the doctor left the room, my legs slipped out from underneath me, literally, as I fell to the floor. I managed to climb back up to my feet.

"Emm! Let me explain," she begged.

I looked at her for only a brief moment, my heart dropping to my uterus. "No, babe. I now know why you had such urgency to turn my brother over. You cheated--and don't even try to give me that shit, that we wanted kids and marriage. We hadn't talked about that for months, and when we had, we planned to move to Alabama, start fresh, get married, and then have kids. You betrayed me in so many ways!"

"But wait! You don't understand! This baby is your ...." Judy began frantically to explain, but I interrupted.

"You're such a bitch! I'm done! And I hope you lose that kid like I just lost my brother!" I walked away and began my search for my actual family, my brother, my blood.

Chapter Seven – Trapped

Blackbird

Awoken by feathers

Swept across her face

A tickle of trickling blood

Thrust to keep the pace

Clumsily bouncing chaos

A new predator arrived

Blocking alternate passage

Irrelevant dead or alive

The scene again infected

Another presence appeared

Escape hatch opened

The protected safely cleared

Angel on 5th Floor

Nurse Henson walked aggressively into the room. She slid back the heavy drapes with force and turned with her hands propped up on her thick hips to cast a glare. "It is a beautiful day today. Rayssa, I said it is a beautiful day!" Rayssa sat up in the bed and held her forearm over her head, shading her eyes from the bright sun. The I.V. dangled from the back of her hand down her nose. Her pale blue eyes watered as she tried to bring Nurse Henson and her white scrubs into focus in front of that piercing halo of light around her. Nurse Henson made her way over to the bed and flung the thin white blankets off her. She repeated, "Miss Rayssa! I said, it is a beautiful day today, a beautiful day to be .... discharged! Come on, girl, you are outta here!" She spoke with excitement, pointing her thumb up in the air and then over her shoulder to the door.

"Are you for real? That last test came back negative?" Rayssa perked up, a huge grin across her ivory face.

"Yes, child! You are finally virus-free! I told you, you would beat this thing! I'm so proud of you. I knew you were a warrior! I have to admit, though, I will miss you," she said, walking to the end of the bed to grab her chart.

Rayssa wiggled her legs in the bed and spun around, anxious to get dressed. "Yay! This is great! I can't wait to get out of here!" Her legs swung over the edge of the bed.

Nurse Henson rushed over to her and placed her hand on her shoulder. "Now, wait just a minute. We still have to unplug and de-needle you! Silly girl." She raised the head of the bed and propped up the pillows. She then assisted by holding Rayssa's I.V. out of the way and nudged her to pull her legs back up on the bed. "Yes, you are going home, but there are some things we need to take care of first. Like I said, someone will be in to remove your I.V. and those old sticky pads from your chest. Next, we will have to wait until your mom gets here to go over instructions and medications after leaving. Then we will have to wait for the doctor to stop by for one final exam and get his signature on the discharge papers."

"Geez, that will take all day!" Rayssa grumbled. "Maybe you shouldn't have told me just yet." Her smile turned into a frown as she grabbed for her cell phone from the small table on wheels beside her bed.

"Yeah, it probably will take most of the day. However, this means no more I.V. or EKG pads and, more importantly... no more special diet! I can sneak you in whatever you'd like! It's on me! Well, within reason anyway," she said while making her way to the door. "I'm calling my Door Deal order in for lunch around 11:30, so be quick in choosing what you would like! I'll be back in a few minutes." She smiled and waved as she exited the room.

Rayssa, a little disappointed that she would have to wait, was still excited about getting to go home. She leaned back on the pillows that Nurse Henson had fluffed and stacked up for her, with her pink, rhinestone cell in hand. An odd, muffled ringtone filled the room as she Chap-Chat-called her bestie, Brae, to tell her the good news but got no answer. *That's really weird. We always talk at this time of the morning, just before our first online class. Maybe she's just in the bathroom.* So she sent her a text.

Dang girl! Y U not answer me?

Call me back

I have great news!

While she waited for Brae to call her back, she took a selfie on Chap-Chat with a date/location stamp that read,

Streaks! Feelin Fire Vibes 2Day!

@ Kanawha County Hospital - March 22, 2025

Then clicked Post.

Post Failed

Please try again later.

What the heck? She laid her phone on her lap and grabbed the yellow, plastic cup of water from the table. She sipped while tugging a cream-colored cable toward her that held the TV remote on the end. *Where is everyone this morning? Figures, I'm finally over this freaking virus, and the world has ended.* She giggled out loud and turned on the TV. Most of the channels had been blocked, displaying a black screen. She stopped on the RLV (Real Life Videos) channel when she saw a video of a cat chasing its tail, then falling off the tailgate of an old pick-up truck. *Maybe there was a storm or something that knocked the satellite out.* She set the cup back on the table and picked her phone up; there were still no replies.

Moments later, an orderly came in. "Hey, Dan!" Rayssa said to the dark, heavy-set man in green scrubs.

"How you doing today, Rayssa? I hear you beat the heat and are going home. That's great, kiddo!" he said.

"Yeah, thanks! But my TV isn't working, can you fix it?" she replied.

He stopped at the foot of her bed and looked up at the TV. "Well, looks like it's working to me," he said as he laughed. "Actually, I heard the TV on, so I knew you were awake. Thought I'd pop in to say Hey and see if you need anything."

Rayssa started surfing through the channels to show Dan that most of them were blank. "Well, see? All the channels are out," she answered.

Dan flipped his hand in the air at the TV as if shooing a fly, "Aw, they've probably just put a blocker on them again. They do that once in a while here in the pediatric ward. Especially during non-visitation hours. That's so the hospital doesn't get sued for the little ones watching something they shouldn't," he said, chuckling.

"That's something else; I'm nearly eighteen. Why did they

stick me in here with all these little kids anyway?" she asked.

"Sorry about that, kid, but you are still underage and considered a minor. But you are in a different section than the young ones. Besides, you're leaving soon anyway!" He answered.

Rayssa sighed, "Yeah, I suppose."

Dan asked before leaving, "So you sure you don't need anything?"

"Is there something going on? I mean, other than the all of sudden block on the channels? It seems my phone may not be working either. None of my friends are answering me," she said, waving her phone in the air.

"Rayssa, don't you worry about a thing. You good, girl! I gotta go." The orderly quickly made his way to the door and pointed back at her, "I'm proud of ya, kid. You're a fighter for sure!" Then he left the room.

After her little chat with Dan, Rayssa was feeling even more certain something was wrong. *Why haven't I heard from my mom yet, much less any of my friends*? She turned back to her phone for answers. She sent Brae another text and then finally one to her mother.

Mom, they say I'm getting out today!

Where you at?

Call me?

About an hour passed when the phone in her room rang. It was her mother, Sylvia. "Hey, baby doll. How are you feeling this morning?"

Rayssa's voice had a trimmer of anxiety. "Mom! Where you at? What's going on?"

Sylvia answered, "The hospital called and said your test was negative and they are going to let you come home! Isn't that great news? I'm coming right over to pick you up."

"Yeah, they told me that! That's great! But Mom, something is wrong. None of my friends are messaging me back, the TV stations are blocked, and everyone is acting weird. What's going on?" she asked.

"I'm on my way, baby. I'll explain everything when I get there. Hold tight, I'll get you out of there asap!" her mother stated calmly.

The secret everyone had been keeping was more severe than she could imagine. Everyone knew about the virus outbreak. It has been the hot topic for over a year. Rayssa herself had just beaten it, and local authorities claimed it had been contained to the state's tri-county area. The broadcasts were already claiming victory. In fact, two other counties had no new cases in the last 30 days. The infection rate had been declining. Yet during the previous twenty-four hours, there seemed to have been an outrageous infection rate within the hospital staff.

When Sylvia arrived at the hospital to pick up Rayssa, she managed to slip through the security cracks just before the entire hospital went on lockdown. However, she was stopped and questioned. She had to provide her I.D. and go through a temperature check. Those who had a fever were escorted by men in hazmat suits to a different location. She was corralled into a waiting area with others and given a number as if she were waiting in line at a famous New York deli. No matter how many questions she asked, demands to see her daughter, and the escalation of her vocal dissatisfaction, she was told repeatedly to sit and wait.

So far, all that was explained was that due to the potentially high rate of transmission, they put the 5th-floor pediatrics on lockdown. Accepting defeat, Sylvia found a not-so-stained chair to sit in, just under a TV attached high above on the wall. She pulled out her phone and sent a text to her daughter Rayssa.

I'm here, baby doll.

I don't know what's going on,

but they won't let me up there to see you just yet.

I will find a way.

Hang in there.

We'll be out of here soon.

Love You!

After hitting send, she got a notification just seconds later.

Message could not be delivered.

Please check the number and try again.

WTF! Why wouldn't it go through? I just paid the stupid bill! She decided to test the service by texting Rayssa's dad, who was clearly outside of the hospital.

Hey Ray,

I'm at the hospital to pick up Rayssa,

but my texts won't go through to her

and something weird is going on.

She stared at her phone while waiting impatiently for his reply. Meanwhile, she noticed people gathering near her in a circle staring at the TV above her head. It wasn't the show that was on, but the news ticker running along the bottom of the screen.

KANAWHA COUNTY HOSPITAL IS ON LOCKDOWN.

A POTENTIAL CRIMINAL MAY BE WREAKING MAYHEM INSIDE.

KANAWHA COUNTY HOSPITAL ON TEMPORARY
LOCKDOWN DUE TO AN UNIDENTIFIED PERPETRATOR.

STAY TUNED FOR FURTHER DETAILS.

Just like a tick that just keeps sucking at the same bite over and over, the message continued to repeat. Sylvia's phone vibrated. *Finally!* Unlocking her cell's screen with her thumbprint, hoping it was Rayssa, she saw the notification. It was Ray, her ex. She opened his text with a sigh.

Holy shit!

I was hoping you already got her!

That place has gone freaking mad!

Sylvia's emotional radar went from extreme nervousness to freaking-out scared as she typed.

WTF u talking about?

What's going on?

Ray began to blow up her phone with a series of texts:

Get her the hell out of there!

The entire hospital is on lockdown.

What? Why?

Rumor has it

that some crazy ass

who became infected is looking for revenge.

They say he lost his wife,

A nurse who worked there,

and his son, an infected patient.

He's blaming the hospital

for his wife contracting the virus and spreading it to his son.

He's blaming the hospital for their deaths.

Now that he's infected too,

he sent an email to the media

saying he no longer had anything to fight for

so he was taking others down with him.

OMG!

He's lost his damn mind!

And he's running loose in that hospital.

Get her out!

Her hands dropped into her lap while clenching her cell so tight as if rigor mortis had just set in. Her hands shook against the torn jeans that she and her daughter bought together to match just weeks ago. She watched, with her mouth agape, as people began to push and shove each other, bombarding the nurse's station. Men screaming and waving their fists, women crying and collapsing against the counter, and some to their knees in prayer. Others began to physically fight among themselves, throwing punches to decide who would see the doctor next.

Holy shit, this is stuff you only see in the end of days kind of movies. What the hell is wrong with people? I need to see my Rayssa. I need to get her out of here. Clearly, fist fighting with others and storming the nurse's station isn't going to get me upstairs. So, Sylvia sat in that chair and pondered on a plan.

Meanwhile, on the fifth floor, Nurse Thatcher came bouncing into the room as bubbly as always and asked, "Hey, girlie, you ready to get that I.V. out?"

"Definitely," she said, placing her arm up on the side rail of the bed for easier access. "So, Dan told me they had blocked some of the channels on the TV. Is that just on this floor? Did they block the cell signal too?"

"Yeah, sorry. The pediatric floor is always the first to go

on lockdown in an emergency." Nurse Thatcher gasped, realizing she had just informed an underage patient there was something so wrong that the hospital was undergoing a lockdown.

"What?" Rayssa's voice shrieked, "We're on lockdown? Why? What's going on?"

As Nurse Thatcher slid the I.V. out of Rayssa's arm, she looked at her with great concern and replied, "I'm really not allowed to say. I've already said too much. I could lose my job."

Rayssa grabbed her hand. "Please. If we are in danger, I have a right to know! Besides, it's not like I'm some little kid!"

Nurse Thatcher placed her hand on Rayssa's shoulder to direct her to lie back against the pillows. "I'm going to pull your gown down, just enough to remove the EKG pads from your chest." While gently removing the pads, she leaned close to her ear, saying softly, "They say there is a man loose that is spreading the virus to all of the staff. But they haven't found him yet. You cannot let anyone know you know." She watched Rayssa's jaw drop open, and her eyes opened as wide as canning jars. "Don't be afraid. You are on the safest floor of this hospital. All the doors are locked, and the elevators have been shut down. No one is getting up here."

After all of Rayssa's tubes and pads were removed, she sat back up in the bed. Drawing her knees into her chest and hugging her legs, she asked, "Shouldn't we be evacuating then?"

While disposing of the needle and pads, Nurse Thatcher patted her on the back and said, "You can get dressed now. Your clothes are in the wardrobe." Moving around to the other side of her bed to unplug the EKG from the wall, she whispered, "No one is allowed in, and no one is leaving because they haven't figured out exactly who might be infected. Just sit tight, sweetie. Everything will be okay."

"So why did you guys tell me I'm going home? That's bullshit! On top of that, you block my cell phone signal so I can't even talk to anyone!" she whined, throwing her phone on the bed.

"We didn't realize the seriousness of the situation until a little while ago. In fact, they just recently told us. I can get you a code to hack the block on the cell signal. There's nothing I can do about the TV." Patting her on the knee, she said, "I'll be back shortly, but you cannot let anyone know you know. Now go ahead and get dressed," she said, exiting the room.

Rayssa got dressed and stood in the doorway of her room, looking down the hall. The nurses' station was two doors down and around the corner. She couldn't see anyone, but she overheard them talking. Nurse Thatcher was at it again, spreading confidential information. "I'm not taking that vaccine. Did you not hear about that patient on the third floor? I think her name was Rachel Morris. Anyway, they said she took the vaccine, became deathly ill, was rushed in here by an ambulance, and died of a brain hemorrhage!"

Rayssa heard Dan approaching the nurses' station. He was easy to detect because he jingled like a big horse adorned with a sleigh bells strap because of all of the keys he carried. "Thatcher! Don't be telling everyone that crap! People are scared enough as it is!" She shrugged her shoulders at him and turned the corner to go back down the hall to Rayssa's room. Rayssa rushed to jump back onto her bed.

Once in the room, Nurse Thatcher handed Rayssa a sticky note with the code and directions on how to unlock the block. "You will have to be more stealthy than that if you're planning on snooping around. Tear this up and flush it when you get through, so no one knows you have the code," she stated firmly and then left the room once again. Rayssa immediately began cracking the block on her phone. The first text she sent out was to her mother.

Mom, are you here?

I know what's going on.

They have had the signal blocked to this floor

I couldn't text until now.

> Yes, baby, I'm here.
>
> I'm downstairs.
>
> They won't let me come up there.
>
> So you do know about the guy here?

Yes, one of the nurses spilled it by accident.

How are we going to get out of here?

> I'm not sure yet
>
> They have been putting people in groups.
>
> They keep taking them to different areas of the hospital.
>
> So it's finally thinning out down here.
>
> Wait, the police are here. Maybe they found him.

The long pause in her mother's texts gave Rayssa time to check messages from her friends and log on to the news updates. They still hadn't found him, but they did discover a hypodermic needle in one of the locker rooms for the staff. The news reported that they traced the virus transmitted throughout the hospital to the automatic air fresheners. The man in question had been injecting a strain of the virus via his blood into the cotton tops of the air fresheners. Since they were motion-activated, each time a staff member would walk through the locker rooms, they were showered not just with a lovely fragrance but also spores from his infected blood.

She copied and pasted the link from the news feed and sent it to her mother.

Did you see this?

> Yeah,

they just now showed it on the news down here.

Mom, we have to get out of here

I don't want this crap again!

I know, I'm working on it.

Rayssa decided she needed to conduct her own investigation. She grabbed a face mask from the box on the wall and some latex gloves. She slipped them on and headed down the hall. Stopping just at the corner near the nurses' station, she peeked around to see if anyone was there. Nurse Henson was on the phone telling someone on the other end that she would have Dan double-check the stairwell doors to ensure they were all locked. She then hung up and left the station in search of Dan.

Rayssa darted past the opening of the hallway, walking toward the opposite end. She glanced into the rooms and saw the younger children in their beds. As she neared the exit sign over the door to one of the stairwells, she saw the NICU. Staring through the large glass window, she teared up. She placed the palm of her hand against the glass and said a little prayer for the tiny baby in the incubator. He wore a little blue knit cap, EKG pads, and a mask with a ventilator. *Hang in there, little man. God, please watch over and protect him.*

"Rayssa!" Dan yelled as he walked swiftly down the hall. "What are you doing? You need to go back to your room and close the door!"

She began walking toward him, "Why, what's going on?"

As they met in the middle of the hallway, he gently grabbed her elbow, saying, "Just, please! Go back to your room, shut the door and stay there."

"Is he up here?" she asked.

Dan's face was full of surprise. "How did you know about him?" He shook his head, placed his trembling hand on her back, nudging her back toward her room. "Doesn't matter how you know. They say he's trying to get up here. So go back to your room and stay put!"

"Where are the nurses?" Rayssa asked. "I mean, I heard Nurse Henson on the phone earlier, but I haven't seen or heard anyone else but you. Where is everyone? What about the kids?"

"It seems he started on this floor yesterday. He hit the locker rooms here on the 5th floor first, then the 6th and 7th floors. The staff from this floor are quarantined in rooms on the other side, in the green wing. So, you need to get to your room and stay there!" Dan nudged her again and continued toward the exit near the NICU.

Rayssa returned to her room, but she stood just inside, peeking out instead of closing the door. The struggle began. Rayssa watched as Dan tried to hold the door closed while someone was trying to pull it open. The horizontal metal bar slipped out from his fingers. A man's arm came through the doorway, holding a taser that connected with Dan's chest. His body shook as if he was having a seizure, then he fell to the floor.

The man stepped into the hallway. He was dressed in scrubs and was wearing a white coat like the doctors. Being a large man, Dan's tolerance level was high; despite being down, he was not done. He swung his leg around, tripping the perpetrator. As he too hit the ground, the taser went flying down the hall. The two men struggled for dominance, exchanging punches. Dan managed to get back to his feet and kicked the perp in the ribs a couple of times. He then leaned over to grab him, pulled him up, and threw two hard right hooks to his face.

As Dan dragged him down the hall, away from the NICU, Rayssa saw the man pull a syringe from his pocket. "Dan! Watch out! He has a needle!" she shouted. As Dan turned to look at Rayssa, he was stabbed in the leg. The perp managed to inject him with the entire contents before snapping the needle off in his leg.

Dan growled out fiercely, "Not on my watch, Mother Fucker!" He then threw the guy against the wall and started whaling on him. The violent fight cast them into the corridor in front of the nurses' station. Rayssa quickly left her room, rushing down the hall. She stopped at each room collecting the children, and escorted them into the NICU. There was still one person on duty in that unit; Nurse Vada was sitting at a desk in the back. Rayssa explained to her what had happened, then grabbed a few blankets and threw them on the floor of a storage room, instructing the children to sit down inside. Afterward, she assisted Nurse Vada in moving the baby boy's incubator away from the window, positioning him beside the desk.

Rayssa sat down for a minute beside her at the desk. "I can't believe this is really happening. Call 911 and let them know he's up here," she said as she pulled out her phone to check her messages. She had finally received replies from her friends, but the only one she opened was from her mother.

I found an unlocked door in the stairwell

I'm coming up

No!!!!

Mom, don't come up here!

He's up here!

There was no reply. Worried about her mother and Dan, Rayssa snuck back out of the NICU and down the hall. Cautiously looking around the corner to the nurses' station, she saw Dan lying on the floor. She knelt beside him and checked for a pulse; it was there, slow and faint, but it was there. The man in the doctor's coat had disappeared. He was not on this side of the floor, so he must have been searching the green wing for the rest of the staff.

160

She went behind the counter looking for something to prop the heavy stairwell door open for her mother. All she could find was some medical tape, bandages, individually wrapped needles, etc., on a cart. *The cart would be too noisy and not at all discreet. The tape,* recalling how her mother had temporarily fixed her bedroom door from getting stuck shut by affixing tape over the latch. *This will work, but what about Dan? I can't just leave him lying here.* She walked back around to where he was. Not seeing any puddles of blood or types of deadly blows, she was curious as to what was in that syringe. *It had to be something other than just the virus to take Dan down that quick.*

Each thought in her head triggered a new one. Flashes of memories began playing like an old projector on a sheet. Her brother Greg was studying Criminal Justice, specifically forensics. He wanted to work in a crime lab where they researched how an actual murder or struggle could have occurred. During this time, he enticed Rayssa to do experiments with him, one being the most effective way to move a dead body. During that trial-and-error event, she learned that a more petite person could not move a large person by their hands. The only way without assistance was to drag them by the feet.

So Rayssa positioned her backside between Dan's feet and raised his legs to rest somewhat on her hips, and began to drag him behind the counter of the nurses' station. That was about as far as she could get him anyway. She then darted across the hall into the other side of the wing to grab some blankets from a storage closet. While bringing them back, she noticed bloody fingerprints on the edge of the counter. The perp was still active, wounded most likely, but active. She placed one blanket under Dan's head and the other one over his body. Then she grabbed the tape and headed back down the hall to the exit.

She taped the latch in the open position so when the door closed, it would not engage in the frame. That way, if her mother came up those stairs, she could get in. She then went back into the NICU ward to check on the other kids and see if the nurse had gotten through to 911. "Did you talk to anyone?"

"Yes, they said they were aware of our situation and were working on the safest method to apprehend him. What did you find?' the nurse asked.

"It's a long story, but Dan is down, and all the other staff are on the other side of the floor. Have you been in the locker rooms in the last two days?" Rayssa answered and questioned her.

She looked puzzled at Rayssa and told her she didn't think so. Rayssa said, "Okay, well, try to keep your distance from the kids, keep your mask and gloves on, and stay here quietly. I'm going to go make sure the air fresheners on this floor have been removed." She left the NICU ward again. While sneaking back down the hallway to the staff lounge and locker room, she regretted not sticking to her Jujitsu classes. *That stuff could come in handy right now. Let's see, how did it go .... Eyes!* As she made duck beaks with her fingers, jabbing the air in front of her, *Ears!* she clapped, imagining a head in between her hands. *Nose!* The palm of her right hand thrust up in the air, into an imaginary nose. She then twisted her hand sideways, holding it flat, and sliced through the air. *Throat!*

She cleared the staff's lounge and locker rooms of all air fresheners, ripping them off the walls. She tossed the containers into a biohazard bin lined with plastic, then rolled it into an empty patient room, pushed it into the bathroom, and closed the door behind her. She removed her gloves and mask, shoving them into the biohazard bin on the wall, washed her hands at the sink, then sat down on the bed. She pulled her phone from her pocket to see if her mother had replied, no answer. She sent her another text.

Mom!

Where are you?

Are you Ok?

Again, no reply. She opened her Chap-Chat from Brae. It was a short clip of a news report on her TV of the hospital hostage situation, then the camera flipped back to her friend's face and dark hair twisted up in a bun. Brae hesitated on the video, then finally asked, "ARE U OK?"

Rayssa opened a live video chat with Brae. "Hey, girl, I'm ok, but he is on this floor. I've gathered all of the kids and put them in a storage room in the back of the NICU. Mom said she was coming up the stairwell, but I haven't seen her, and she won't text me back, so I'm worried about her. All the staff was quarantined on the other side of the floor, and Dan fought with the dude and lost. I drug him behind the nurses' station. I've dismantled all of the air fresheners, but I'm not sure what to do next."

"Oh my gosh! That is crazy! Please be careful! Just wait for the police to get up there." Brae replied with such immense tension in her voice.

"I don't know, girl. The last nurse is in the NICU with the kids. She said the police told her that they knew he was up here and were trying to figure out a safe way to catch him," Rayssa whispered back. "I think I better go. I need to pay attention in case he comes back this way. Text my dad, call the police, let them know what's going on, and have them find my mom!"

"Dang, ok! I'm on it!" Brae announced with assurance, "I got you! Be careful!"

Rayssa put on a clean mask and gloves and then sauntered down to the nurses' station. She knelt beside Dan, rechecking his pulse, which seemed to be getting weaker. His breathing had become more sporadic; on occasion, he would stop, then became very labored. *He won't last much longer like this. Think, think, think!* Using a couple of the bandages from the cart, she dabbed the sweat from his face. "Hang in there, Dan; we are fighters, remember?" *I have to do something. What was that stuff they gave people who overdosed?* Turning her phone on silent, she then sent Brae a text.

I'm going after him!

This has gone on long enough!

Rayssa! No! Don't!

Dan is going to die if I don't!

I have to at least find something

Or someone to help him!

I don't think he injected the virus into him

Because this guy is not a big man like Dan

He should have been no match

He had to have drugged him!

Ok

Narcan!

Find some Narcan!

That's what they gave my cousin

when he OD'd!

 ok!

Creeping around to the other side of the counter, she checked both directions of the hall of the green wing, where the staff had been quarantined, and the perp had disappeared. Moving quickly, she found the supply closet for that side of the floor and darted inside as quietly as possible. She began searching the shelves and found a box that read Narcan, and she grabbed a couple of the blistered packs containing a weird-looking nasal spray.

Stuffing the packets into her pocket, she twisted around to take one final look around. Among the bedpans, bandages, boxes of gloves, and masks, she saw a few bags that looked like an oversized version of her dad's leather-travel toiletry bag. She pulled one over to the edge of the shelf, unzipped it, and took a look inside; her lips sprang into a big grin. She zipped it back up, snatched that one and one more from the shelf, and eagerly checked the hall before dashing back over to Dan.

Brae, being the star softball player, would have been proud of the way she slid in behind the counter beside Dan as if she had just slid into home plate. She pulled the Narcan packets from her pocket, and as she ripped one open, she heard Dan gasp for breath and then stopped. *Oh shit! I'm too late! Am I too late?* "Dan!" she yelled with chills and a racing heart. She popped her head up from behind the counter to see if anyone was coming. *Did he hear me?* With a sigh and shaky hands, she administered the nasal spray to Dan. He still wasn't breathing. She clenched her fist high above her head, slammed them both down onto Dan's ample chest, and cried, "Don't you dare leave me!"

He gasped again. Rayssa looked over each shoulder, back at him, then the clock, repeatedly, for what seemed like half an hour. Yet, within minutes he opened his eyes. "Rayssa? What happened? Where did he go?"

Scrunching her thin eyebrows together and waving her hand up and down, signing to him to keep it down, she whispered, "He's still up here."

Dan sat up and leaned against the wall. Taking one of the nurse's thermoses from under the counter, she had a sip and gave the rest to him. He picked up the empty Narcan canister from the floor, wiggled it in front of her, and said, "Smart kid! Thanks!" She then pulled one of the bags around in front of them and unzipped it. "Yes, you are indeed a smart kid; those are the emergency tactical bags."

As Dan pulled out a sealed pouch of surgical tools, they heard a loud crash. Rayssa jumped to her feet and ran over to the corner of the station. She saw the perp dragging one of the nurses down the hall by her arm. It was Nurse Henson being pulled, leaving a bloody skid mark behind her limp body. Rayssa ducked quickly out of sight, just a little too late. He spotted her, dropping Nurse Henson to bolt over to her. "He's coming!" she screamed as she ran back toward Dan. Still weak, he staggered a bit, trying to stand and steady himself. The perp grabbed Rayssa by the throat, lifting her into the air. She pulled her thoughts together, *Do it! Do it, dumbass! You just practiced it moments ago!* She let go of his arms and boxed his ears while kicking him in the groin, just like Sensei had taught her years ago. He dropped her and fell to his knees.

Dan had grabbed one of the scalpels from the pack he pulled out of the bag and lunged over toward them. The perp stood up to meet Dan's swing, blocking him with his forearm. While Dan swung again with his other hand, Rayssa, who was still on the ground holding her throat, swept his knee. As the perp began to fall on top of Rayssa, Dan caught him in the throat with the scalpel, pushing him backward. Rayssa crawled away from him, where he now lay on the floor. With each breath he took, blood gurgled out from around the scalpel stuck in his throat.

Dan looked at Rayssa and motioned for her to toss him the emergency bag. "Are you ok?"

She slid the opened bag over to him. "Yes, I'll be fine, but now I have to go find my mom! She said she was coming up one of the stairwells, but I haven't seen her, and she hasn't replied."

Using the bag's sterile pads, he removed the scalpel from the man's throat and applied pressure. "Go! Go, find your mom!" He nodded in understanding. "Take the other bag, just in case!"

Rayssa grabbed the bag and ran full speed down the hallway. She paused just long enough to throw the NICU door open to yell, "The perp is down. Tell the police it's safe to come up now!" She then popped open the exit door that she had taped earlier. There her mother was, lying passed out on the next landing down. She slid down the handrail to her with the bag in hand. "Mom! Are you ok? Mom!" She dropped to her knees and pulled her mother over onto her back. Sylvia was in the same condition Dan had been in. However, she was not breathing at all. "Oh, Lord! Please help us!" she cried out in a panicked plea. Frantically digging through the bag, she happened to find another Narcan package. Ripping it open, she realized it was a syringe instead of the nasal spray. *I don't know how to do this! Oh please, God, help me! What do I do?* Taking a chance, she pulled the plastic protective cap off the needle, squirted a bit of the medicine in the air, then stabbed it in her mother's upper thigh.

She pulled the torso of her mother's body up onto her lap. Tears streamed down her face, making it difficult for her even to see. "Mom! Please come back. I need you!" As Rayssa squeezed her mother from behind, just under her breasts, Sylvia finally took a gasp of air. Rayssa knew her pulse was still feeble, and her breathing was not consistent. *It didn't take this long for Dan to come to. I don't know what to do.* "Lord, please! I'm begging you, save her!" Rayssa swept the hair back from her mother's pale ghostly face and saw her eye was swollen and red, along with a busted mouth. *She must have put up one hell of a fight.* "I'm not going to let you go that easy!" She pulled out the other packet of Narcan Nasal spray that she had stuck in her pocket. *It couldn't hurt at this point.* Holding her mother steady on her lap with one hand, she tore the packet open with her teeth and squirted the canister into her nose. "I love you!"

A few extremely long minutes passed before Sylvia's breathing stabilized, and she opened her eyes. After a few deep breaths, she mustered up softly, "I l o v e y o u t o o." By this time, the police finally arrived. They cleared the stairwell, and the EMTs placed Sylvia on a backboard and took her down to the E.R. for further care and observation. Rayssa showed the police where she had hidden the children and led the others down the hall to the nurses' station, where Dan sat in a puddle of blood on the floor beside the perp's dead body.

One crew came in to take Dan down to the E.R., as it is said that Narcan wears off and must be continually administered for a while afterward. It seems the dose Rayssa gave him was just enough to save his life and for him to save hers. Another group of EMTs removed the perp's body as well as Nurse Henson's, while another team of police officers searched the rooms for the remaining staff.

After a week of investigations and sterilizations of the scene, the reporters were finally given the details of the event that took place. Newspapers ranging from the small city to other countries headlined the breaking news:

SEVENTEEN-YEAR-OLD GIRL AND MEDICAL ORDERLY
FROM KANAWHA COUNTY HOSPITAL SAVES A
MULTITUDE OF LIVES FROM A MASS MURDERER

Rayssa LaFleur, age 17, saved 15 children, a nurse, an orderly, her mother, and most likely countless more on March 22, 2025, when a mass murderer, Benjamin Pitman, entered the Kanawha County Hospital late in the evening of March 21, 2025. Using his diabetic syringes, he extracted his own infected blood and began injecting the deadly virus into the air fresheners located in the hospital staff's lounges and locker rooms.

Mr. Pitman had previously released a statement to a local paper that his plan was already in progress. He said he was seeking revenge for his wife contracting the virus while working at the hospital, who in turn brought it home and infected their 6-year-old son. He wanted to inflict the same illness and pain on those responsible for making his wife sick and the pediatric staff for allowing his son to die.

Two hundred thirty people were infected by his malevolent anarchy, while 26 people lost their lives and seven are still in critical condition.

Dan Matting fought Mr. Pitman, which resulted in his being stabbed with a hypodermic needle full of morphine, eventually immobilizing him. However, because of his bravery, Miss LaFleur was able to gather the 14 children on her floor into the NICU ward, warn the nurse, and assist in hiding the children and moving a newborn's incubator out of sight.

Names of victims and Story continued on page 4

On April 22, 2025, one month later to the day, Rayssa was invited as a special guest of the United States of America's President Janie Calleen and First Man, Arron Calleen. She was accompanied by her mother, after making a full recovery. During her visit to the White House, she was given the highest civilian award, The Presidential Medal of Freedom. Dan was also invited as a special guest who had been acknowledged and awarded the second-highest civilian honor, The Presidential Citizens Medal.

On the plane back home, Rayssa looked across the aisle to Dan and said, "Everyone says I'm a hero, but I don't feel like one. So many people still lost their lives."

Dan reached across the aisle and grabbed her hand. "Yes, you are a hero. You saved all of those kids, the NICU nurse, your mom, and me! Not to mention all the other people you protected by taking down all the air fresheners on that floor. You deserve all of this and more!"

She gently pulled her hand away and leaned her chair back. "Yeah, maybe, but … you should have received the Presidential Medal of Freedom too or better yet, instead of me, because you nearly lost your life. If you really think about it, we all survived because you took him down!"

Sylvia laid her hand on Rayssa's knee, leaned over so she

could make eye contact with Dan, and spoke confidently, "You are both heroes! None of us would be here if it hadn't been for both of you!" Looking back and forth between the two of them, she continued, "Hell, in fact, you guys probably saved the whole damn country by administering that Narcan to Dan and me. That's how they discovered Narcan didn't just combat the narcotic he injected us with but also slowed and in most cases blocked the effects the virus had on the respiratory and nervous system." She leaned back in her chair with the biggest grin on her face. "My baby isn't just a hero but a legend!"

Dan leaned back, raised both arms above his head, and interlaced his fingers while rubbing his bald head. Looking back to Rayssa, he said, "On that day, on the 5th floor, you weren't just a hero, you weren't just a legend; girl, you were my angel!" Rayssa pulled the hard resin case holding her newly awarded medal from her inner jacket pocket and gazed upon it with a smile, finally accepting a bit of the glory.

Afterword

The picture above was a selfie taken by the author in March 2020, using a Snapchat filter, when the lockdowns in the USA began. During this time the stories in this book came to life and were inspired by this image. Although all tales are fictional, they were created as means of coping while living through the experience of a pandemic.

Throughout this book there were mentions of drug and alcohol use, attempted rape, attempted suicide, murder, and more. It is London Blue's wish that if you are experiencing addictions of any kind, any thoughts of harming yourself or others that you please seek help. In a world where some still frown on mental health issues, let it be known there is help out there!

Please do not give in and never give up! Keep fighting the good fight!

Much ♥

Need Help?

Addiction Assistance

Stopaddiction.us

Free Call & Consultation

1-877-578-6624

SAMHSA

https://www.samhsa.gov/find-help/national-helpline

1-800-662-HELP (4357)

Suicide Prevention

Call the National Suicide Prevention Lifeline
1-800-273-8255

OR

Text GO to 741741 to reach a trained Crisis Counselor
through Crisis Text Line, a global not-for-profit
organization. Free, 24/7, confidential.

Crisis Text Line -- Text Hello to 741741

Sexual Assault Assistance

https://RAINN.org
1-800-656-HOPE (4673)
https://victimconnect.org or Hotline: 1 (800) 799 – 7233

Available 24 hours a day, 7 days a week,
via phone and online chat.

ABOUT THE AUTHOR

London Blue

Living in a real haunted house as a child, London Blue became interested in horror at a very young age. She is a Lifelong resident of Kanawha County, WV, and a proud member of the West Virginia Writer's Group, Horror Writers Assoc. (International), Horror Writers Assoc. - WV Chapter, S.A. Write Club, and the Appalachian Paranormal Investigative Society.

Although she writes fiction and has a Christian background, which you will often see Biblical references in her work, she still leans towards seeking the truth of dark and scary things.

She goes on to say, "Ignorance is what we should truly fear the most."

You can find her on most social media platforms under the handle @wvlondonblue, #wvlondonblue & #wvmaskedmayhem, as well as her website wvlondonblue.com.

Made in the USA
Columbia, SC
12 August 2021